Wild Horse Running

BOOKS WRITTEN AND ILLUSTRATED BY SAM SAVITT

Wild Horse Running
Sam Savitt's True Horse Stories
Equestrian Olympic Sketchbook
America's Horses
A Day at the L.B.J. Ranch
Vicki and the Black Horse
Rodeo: Cowboys, Bulls and Broncos
Around the World with Horses
There Was a Horse
Midnight
Step-a-Bit

Wild Horse Running

Written and illustrated by Sam Savitt

DODD, MEAD & COMPANY
New York

To the memory of my mother and father

Library of Congress Catalog Card Number: 73-2132
ISBN 0-396-06808-1
Printed in the United States of America

Preface

FREEDOM is a relative thing. To a carriage horse, just the release from harness, to stand quietly alone in a straight stall, can be freedom. To the young racing Thoroughbred, freedom might be acres of luscious, fenced-in pastures. But to the wild mustang, freedom is the endless sweep of the land-without-fences. There can be no compromise! He is on his own and will accept no shelter from man. He lives under the big sky, surviving the howling winds and drifting snow of winter, and the blazing heat of summer. He moves lightly through a country of juniper and sage, of deep arroyos and mesas. He drinks water where he can find it, gathered in stagnant pools or running cold and clear through winding, grassy canyons. This brand of freedom is the mustang's heritage.

Part One

1

WHEN he was born, the mustang's color was deep gray, almost black, and all the company he had that April morning was his mother, standing by. His blurry eyes could not see too well, but his nose kept sniffing at his long, sticklike legs, folded in front of him. For almost twenty minutes, his head swiveled about as he studied his surroundings. Then, he tried to stand up. First, he managed to get his front legs unfolded. Next, using his head and neck for leverage, he struggled until he was sitting up like a dog. With a quick heave-ho, he tried to straighten his hind legs in order to support the small bony rump. He did this, too . . . for about three seconds; then the whole works came apart.

His mother, a bay mare, nickered and stepped forward. The foal tried again . . . three times, until he was balanced precariously on four wobbly stems. He attempted to walk—almost went down, but managed to keep right side up by leaning against his mother's belly.

His vision had cleared somewhat, for now he could make out his mother's foreleg. His muzzle pressed against her shoulder.

He was hungry. He poked her hard, not quite knowing where to find food, but instinctively aware that his breakfast was nearby. She cautiously maneuvered her body, swung her nose around, and shoved him into position. He drank ravenously. . . . After awhile, he stepped back. A few drops of milk clung to his tiny mouth.

Following that, the colt moved about awkwardly for almost a half hour, testing his new legs. They were still a bit rubbery in the joints, but were getting stronger by the second. Once he even attempted a short pirouette, and occasionally his hind legs kicked out, as if they had a mind of their own. The cool mountain air, loaded with rich springtime smells, made his nostrils quiver. He cocked his head and his ears flicked forward as a bee

droned by. Later, he found a grassy nook which the rays of morning sunshine had also found and warmed. He collapsed in it, closed his eyes and slept his first sleep—and perhaps dreamed his first dream under the brightening sky.

His mother grazed close by. Occasionally, she raised her head to study the distant landscape. All that could be heard were the sounds of the springtime birds while, high overhead, an eagle circled lazily against a pink cloud.

2

TIME to go! The mare's muzzle whacked her foal hard across the rump early the next morning. Cloud (as he later came to be called) lurched to his feet, then promptly fell flat on his face.

It was time to return to the herd. The mare knew that, if she did not do this soon, the stallion would come looking for her. Only at foaling time was a mare allowed to drop out to be alone —often for hardly a day, until her foal was strong enough to run. She poked Cloud again. This time, the youngster scrambled to a standing position—and stayed up. The mare turned and wove her way down the hill, with her baby at her side.

The foal's vision was much clearer today. The grass, tall and fresh green, tickled his flanks as he moved along. The slope was alive with thousands of spring flowers—reds, yellows, purples, every imaginable color—and clouds of gaily-hued butterflies rose fluttering above them as the mustangs passed by.

The foal trotted awkwardly beside his mother. At first, he stuck pretty close, then gradually, as he gained more confidence, he forged ahead. He grew bolder by the minute. Abruptly, he stopped in his tracks when he became aware of a huge form coming up the hillside toward him. It loomed larger and larger. Fear had not yet become a part of the foal's nature, so he just stood his ground—waiting. The gray stallion came on steadily. He by-passed the foal without a downward glance and brought up in front of the mare. His nostrils blew softly against her brown neck, reassuring himself that she belonged to his band. He was magnificent, steely gray, with light dapples scattered across his flanks and quarters. His head was slightly Roman nosed, but the rest of him had the *quality* look of the Arabian Horse. When he was satisfied with his inspection, he wheeled and loped easily back down the hillside, with the colt and its mother close at his heels.

Before long, young Cloud could see other mares and their foals below. The wild horses were spread out over a wide meadow.

As soon as his mother reached them, she began to chomp huge mouthfuls of the juicy green grass. That reminded him of his own growling stomach. As he nursed, out of the corner of one eye, he watched another mare grazing nearby. Her baby was peeking at him from under her belly.

The gray stallion moved off to high ground. He ate sporadically, constantly raising his head to survey the rim of the valley. Any sound—the snap of a twig, the roll of a pebble—would cause him to pivot sharply, ready to face whatever danger threatened. The day wore on. The mares munched lazily, and the foals nursed, romped, and slept. . . .

A shrill whistle brought Cloud to his feet, like a jack-in-the-box. Almost twenty yards away, the gray stallion cut across his vision. He was trotting—his hoofs barely touching the grass. His tail was straight up like a banner. His head was high and

fierce and his eyes were pinpointed on a black horse galloping toward him. There were no preliminaries to the fight. The stallions met head-on, above the ground, striking forefeet. Their ears were flattened, mouths opened, teeth bared. They crashed like two locomotives, with an impact that seemed to rock the entire landscape. They screamed. Their teeth, slipping off firm flesh, clicked together like steel traps. They came at each other again and again, seeking jugular veins, each one looking for the opening that would enable him to kill or cripple his opponent. Now they whirled with catlike rapidity, and a pair of flying heels hitting against another pair of flying heels cracked like a whipsnap of lightning.

Through all this, Cloud stood frozen, his eyes glued to the battle. The black stallion was the heavier, and once his superior weight crashed the gray horse to the ground. He leaped in, striking down hard to finish his adversary, but the gray rolled away like a sidewinder and was on his feet in a flash, meeting the black shoulder to shoulder before he was able to pursue his advantage. This time, the sheer ferocity of his counterattack sent the dark intruder back on his hocks. The black twisted sideways, to keep from falling, and, at that instant, the gray stallion opened a wide gash on his enemy's flank.

The black began yielding ground but the gray stallion gave him no chance to recover. He bore in, cutting, biting. The battle drifted across the meadow, chopping down anything that grew in its path. Sometimes, when it crossed a sandy stretch, the gladiators were enveloped in boiling dust . . . then they emerged into the open again, like giant sea monsters.

The mares and other foals watched calmly, as if this was a common occurrence, but Cloud was hypnotized. He left his mother's side in order to see better. She called but he paid no attention. He was caught up in this contest for survival. He could not understand why he was so strangely stimulated. Perhaps, in his animal brain, he instinctively felt this was a picture of exciting things to come. Actually, Cloud had no way of knowing about the heritage of the stallion and the mares he led. The colt was not yet aware of how the gray leader guarded his band against all enemies the year round. Keeping them to himself against all opponents had made the gray horse fiercely possessive and domineering.

These things the foal would learn with time. Now he watched the gray stallion come back across the meadow alone. The foe had been vanquished. Sudsy sweat, mixed with blood, covered the gray's shoulders like a mantle of victory. His eyes were still glazed—wild looking. His nostrils were wide, red, blowing hard, and his flanks were heaving from exertion.

Slowly, Cloud returned to his mother. He nursed deeply and lay down exhausted, for had he not just met and fought his first enemy? He closed his eyes and dreamed. Occasionally, he cried out in his sleep, and his long legs jerked convulsively.

3

THE summer passed quickly. During this period, Cloud grew rapidly. He "found his legs," and became ready and agile in the use of them. He learned about the many things which made up his day. He learned that the earth is hard and hurts when one falls on it; that the green grass which grows up out of the ground is good to eat; that water running cold in the mountain streams is good to drink; that certain scents—those of coyote, wolves, and mountain lions—are danger signals. One morning, he followed a porcupine and got several barbs in his muzzle for his pains!

Another time, he was almost pounced on by a cougar when he wandered too far from his mother's side. He was passing beneath a rocky overhang and, if he had not just then shied away from a bird which flew up under his feet, he would have had a huge cat on his back. As it was, the lion landed right smack in front of him. Cloud was so shocked that he tore a hole in the earth as he wheeled and ran out of there so fast his attacker never had a chance for a second try. Live and learn,

good and bad, these were the facts of life. Cloud gained the skill to take them as he met them.

He also witnessed his father fighting again and again. The powerfully built stallion guarded his herd vigilantly, galloping forward to challenge any strange horse that appeared. Usually, a battle followed, and never once was the gray bested. He fought with a kind of merciless ferocity that was thrilling and awful to watch. Sometimes he came back virtually unscathed, but other times he was bloody and bruised, his neck and withers and back painfully lacerated. But he always came back proudly and confidently, fiercely neighing his triumph, making the mesa ring with his defiant challenging of all intruders.

He didn't pay particular attention to Cloud or to any of the other foals. His job was one of leadership and protection for the entire band and he devoted himself to it completely.

The gray foal made friends with other gangling, big-kneed youngsters about his own age. They romped and frolicked over the deep meadows, taking time out only to eat and catnap.

Cloud's first summer on the high plateaus was a happy, carefree existence. He tasted everything that grew and everything seemed to be edible. As the autumn approached, his steely gray coat started to thicken, and cold winds moaned over the mesas at night. The days grew shorter and, one gray morning, a fine white substance came whirling through the air. Cloud blinked his eyes when the flakes snagged on his lashes. He tried to smell them on the ground, but they seemed to evade his probing muzzle. They settled over the field softly and gently. The older horses sniffed the breeze and began soberly to pick their way to lower country. It snowed almost every day now, obliterating the grass with a white blanket which, as time went on, grew deeper and deeper.

The band of horses drifted before the blowing snow. They were not alone, for occasionally, Cloud glimpsed deer and elk traveling in the same direction. Eventually, the migrants reached the lonely banks of a river in the lower country. The stallion halted his group because he knew that, up ahead, were the outlying ranches and barbed wire.

They wintered here. For days at a time, they were forced to stand, their backs humped to the storm. It was extremely hard on the foals. More than once, their bodies were plastered with ice as they hovered to the leeward of their patient mothers. A thick crust formed on the top of the drifts, making it almost impossible for them to paw down to reach the feed underneath. Their small hoofs became tender and raw from the constant digging and, wherever they went, they left red tracks in the white snow. Perhaps, at these times, the foals wondered what had happened to the warmth of the sun and all the good green grass.

The mares took their offspring to the river bank, where they ate willow bark and the few tips that protruded from the thick white blanket. There were several wolves in the area and they shadowed the band constantly. Before the winter was over, the predators managed to bring down two foals, as well as some old horses that were weak from age and exhaustion. The gray stallion drove the wolves off again and again—until he was gaunt and worn and hardly able to stand.

But, finally, the snow turned to slush under Cloud's tender hoofs. The slush turned to water, which ran into the river, leaving green shoots of grass exposed. Then, as if from a bad dream, the band came slowly back to life. Feeding and recuperating as they went, the wild horses began their spring trek back to the high country.

4

BY late spring, the hard winter was forgotten. Cloud was a yearling—he was growing up. The hardships he had suffered had taken a lot out of him but now his ribs and hip bones had disappeared back into his body. The long, dry hairs on his hide began to shed. His tender feet healed and grew firm and flinty. Again, he felt the urge to run and kick up his heels and romp across the green mesas. The stallion resumed his lofty battle station, whistling a challenge to every strange horse that appeared on the horizon.

Each day, the band traveled for miles, feeding as it went, but the older animals seemed more restless than usual and the gray stallion seemed more watchful. The new foals stayed close to their mothers but the yearlings took all this caution and vigilance lightly. They galloped about, racing each other constantly, content that they were invincible and nothing could hurt them.

By August, Cloud was getting the look of his Arabian ancestors. His neck was developing an arch. His mane and tail were lengthening and his coat shone like ancient silver in the

dazzling sunlight. He could run faster than any of the other colts. In their mock battle play, he was always the victor and, what's more, when chased by his "enemies," he could leap across the ravines and windfalls in a way that discouraged all pursuit. How proud and fearless he was!

But the time was coming when Cloud's vanity was to suffer a severe setback. The wild horses had spent a restless night in the protective covering of a clump of aspen. They had been led there yesterday by the gray stallion. Something was in the air! Cloud smelled a scent—strange and unfamiliar. It was neither wolf nor big cat, yet he felt an instinctive dread as it filled his nostrils.

Just before the dawn, the stallion led the jittery herd from the aspen grove. They had hardly cleared the fringe when there was a sharp clatter of hoofs to their right, and three horses carrying strange figures on their backs swept over a rise and down toward the band at a dead run.

There was no mistaking the gray stallion's snort. It was at once a warning and a command. The mares bunched and, seconds later, were in full flight. Cloud panicked completely. He had never seen humans before. Their shouts and yells terrified him. He must get as far away from them as his flashing speed would allow. He fairly flew over the rough and uneven terrain. The running mares were moving too slowly for him. He passed them, bounding over everything and anything in his path like a scared rabbit. He had come up alongside his sire when, like a bolt of lightning, the gray stallion whipped around. His ears were flattened and his mouth was wide open. Cloud almost turned inside out, trying to stop. The leader gave him a glancing blow with one shoulder that sent the yearling scuttling back into the herd. The attack had scared the hysteria right out of him. Soon he realized that these were not panic-stricken horses he was running with. It was an orderly withdrawal, with the stallion leader in command. He knew what he was doing. This was an old game to him.

After the first burst of speed to put the pursuers far behind, the band settled into a steady, easy lope. The miles rolled by. Glancing back through the dust, Cloud could still see the horse hunters, but he was steady now and calmer. His confidence was returning. The running older horses enveloped him in a magic cloak of security which sustained him for the remainder of that day.

Toward evening, the band stopped in a grove of juniper. Their pursuers had been left far behind. The wild horses spent an uneasy night—eating and resting fitfully. Through the long, dark hours, the stallion never ceased to patrol the perimeter of his herd.

At dawn, a rider appeared on the horizon and the wild horses were off again. By mid-day, the rider had dropped out of sight—but simultaneously, off to the band's left, a new rider came into view.

The herd was being relayed. Riders with fresh mounts had been stationed in pre-arranged places. As one pair tired, another took up the chase, allowing the wild horses hardly a moment's rest. Cloud could not understand what was happening, but the gray leader knew. The idea was to exhaust the mustangs—wear them down—and trap them. Nightfall found the horses so weary they could hardly stand, let alone eat.

The pursuit moved relentlessly into the third day. It was late in the afternoon, during one of their infrequent pauses, that a gangling little colt, running at his mother's side, dropped into a patch of gama grass and refused to budge again. When it came time to resume the flight, the mare could not get him to his feet. He was spent, finished. She refused to leave him. The stallion drove her away, but she swung wide and returned to her foal. The stallion raised his head. Their pursuers were close now—the rest of the band was poised for flight. With an angry squeal, he rushed at the colt and killed it with a single snap of his powerful jaws at the base of its skull. Then and only then would the mare leave the spot, for she would never have deserted her foal while it still lived.

On the fourth day, two more foals were killed by the stallion. Several mares dropped out, too leg-weary to move on. The pursuers by-passed them, for it was the stallion leader and the younger horses they wanted. The chase now swung upgrade, through a long draw, then out into the open again. Jagged cliffs, reaching upward on both sides, were funneling the wild horses into the mouth of a narrow canyon.

The gray stallion immediately sensed the trap. Four riders were closing in—two behind and one on each flank of the faltering band. He slid abruptly to a halt, swapped ends, and charged back through his band, frantically trying to reverse them.

But it was too late. Cloud was carried on through like a wood chip on a surging sea. The dust was thick now, but he could hear the shouts of the mustangers and the squeals of terrified horses. He tried to climb the walls of the canyon into which he was being swept but the sides were too slick and steep. A rope slapped him hard alongside his neck and slid off his shoulder. Now terror lent him a fresh burst of energy and, with one mighty lunge, he managed to hook his forefeet over a ledge almost eight feet above him. He strained upward, his breath coming in whistling gasps. His hind legs fought for a hold on

the crumbling rock, then anchored into an outcrop and drove the rest of him on over the ledge. He landed headfirst in a giant fissure. Scrambling to his feet, he raced along it, spotted a narrow ravine to his right, dove into it and up—up—up, reaching, digging in. Rocks and shale tumbled about under him, shooting back down the slope in a rattling cascade that vibrated against the canyon walls like a roll of thunder. But he was free. He had made it!

Beyond the lip of the canyon spread a wide mesa—and across this Cloud flew. Blind panic gave him wings, carrying him over the boulder-strewn ground like a jet before takeoff. After a while, he came down to a stumbling walk . . . and finally stopped.

The yearling was utterly spent. His flanks were working like a bellows and his knees trembled with every breath. He stood swaying, dazed with fatigue, hardly knowing where he was—or how he had reached there. But as his youthful strength returned and his vision cleared, he found himself on a rise of ground overlooking a long valley. A sparkling stream ribboned its way across the green land. Aspen and hemlock marked its course, while on all sides high, jagged cliffs, like great medieval castles, formed a protective wall against all invaders. A beautiful silence permeated the golden afterglow of the setting sun.

The colt watched the evening shadows creep up the canyon walls, and the sky begin to deepen into night. He shivered as a chill breeze brushed his wet flanks. Where had all the horses gone, and where were his mother and the gray stallion? But he was too weary, too exhausted to puzzle about them for long now. Slowly, he collapsed onto the still warm earth. A coyote wailed far off, but Cloud was instantly asleep, oblivious to the nighttime stirrings around him.

5

JUST before dawn, Cloud awoke with a start. He tried to rise but every bone and muscle in his body resisted his efforts. He rolled flat on his side and stretched and flexed his aching neck and legs. Yesterday's mad dash to escape the mustangers had left him battered and hurting all over.

When at last he managed to struggle to his feet, he teetered his way down to the stream. Standing in the middle of it, he drank deeply. He remained there a little while, for the ice-cold water gurgling around his legs cooled his strained and feverish tendons. Later, he satisfied his hunger on the deep green grass that grew everywhere.

After that, he felt better and went to look for his mother and the rest of the herd. He back-tracked along the way he had come for almost an hour but found nothing. He continued to wander on until he came upon a wide gorge that blocked his way. He stood on the ledge and whinnied as loudly as he could. It was a shrill, penetrating sound that lost itself somewhere in the depths of the canyons. There was no answer. In all his short life Cloud had never been without companionship, and because he was a gregarious creature, this awful loneliness persistently gnawed at his insides and spurred him on in his search. He called again and again. . . .

At last, he found a trail leading into the gorge and gingerly made his way downward. It was terribly hot at the bottom, where all the intensity of the midday sun was trapped and held by the blistering stone walls. Vultures circled in the sky, off to his right. He turned in that direction—any company would be welcome. As he drew close to where more of the huge birds were feeding, they hopped awkwardly out of his way, but none flew off. He stretched his neck down and sniffed at what they were eating, then jerked violently back when he recognized one of the colts from his herd. There was the smell of death everywhere. Another carcass lay near the first. Evidently, the animals, in their efforts to escape, had leaped or fallen off the edge of the arroyo and died on the rocks below. Cloud wheeled and rushed out of there as quickly as he could.

Scrambling back up along the trail, he reached the ledge at the top and made his way to where he had spent the night. This place was familiar. Here, somehow, he felt less lonely. He grazed all afternoon, but, every so often, he seemed suddenly to remember something. His head came up then and turned slowly to scan the horizon. His whinnying was softer now, more plaintive, expecting no answer.

Shortly before sunset, the day began to darken. Black storm clouds formed and billowed above the young mustang, blocking out the blue sky. Lightning leaped through them and claps of thunder punctuated the still atmosphere. Then a wind came up. As it increased in velocity, the trees along the stream bent and moaned. Bits of branches and brush whipped crazily across the ground. Cloud bowed his head and moved slowly before the brewing storm. Then the rain came, driving horizontally like the wind. Constantly struck by all kinds of flying debris, he drifted southward for several miles. Water was rushing everywhere, eroding the earth beneath his hoofs, even as he stepped on it.

Finally, Cloud found higher ground and climbed upward. Now he was being pelted unmercifully by hailstones. Ahead of him loomed a wall of rock but, beneath an overhanging shelf, he could make out a dark cavern. No water could reach him here. It was high enough and wide enough to accommodate him, but, once inside the entrance, he instinctively turned to face the outside.

A pebble rolled behind him and, in a flash, he whirled about to face whatever danger threatened. At first, he couldn't see a thing, but, as he peered into the blackness, he made out a shadowy something that strangely resembled the figure of a horse. Stifflegged, he stepped forward, his nostrils dilated, searching. Friend or foe? He heard a soft nicker. It had to be a friend!

The two young horses met nose to nose. Recognition was

instantaneous. They rubbed shoulders and necks and made faces and mouthed each other, as horses will sometimes do when they meet. Everything about them seemed to be crying out how glad they were to see one another.

Horses form extremely strong attachments but, with Cloud and the bay, this devotion was even stronger and ran deeper than in most cases. Both animals had come from the same band, had romped together since they were foals. Both had somehow escaped the mustangers and found each other when they really needed someone to hang on to.

Early the following morning, the pair left their shelter. Cloud led off. The bright bay colt followed at his heels, happy to let the young gray take command. By noon, they reached Cloud's special valley and instantly fell to grazing. They kept at it for over three hours but never once drifted more than ten feet apart. Life was good again. Occasionally, they stopped to look and listen, but already the past was beginning to take its place in the scheme of things for them.

Indian summer was settling over their valley. Color was beginning to show on the tops of the trees—some were already shedding their leaves.

The afternoon was hot for this time of the year. Cloud was slowly picking his way up the side of a steep rocky incline like a mountain goat. At the foot of the slope behind him, the bay was drinking from a tiny spring that gurgled up from the earth.

The gray mustang was searching for tufts of foliage that were still green here—unlike the burned-out vegetation of the valley floor. His velvet lips probed between the crags, catching everything edible, then snatching it up between strong teeth with the precision of grass clippers. So intent was he on his ques

that he failed to notice the long mottled shape stretched out before him.

The rattlesnake was startled and struck with no warning. Cloud reared back. His muzzle whipped to one side, with six feet of diamondback latched to the end of it. The snake let go then and went sailing off into space, turning end over end before it crashed to the rocks below. The sharp pain of the bite passed quickly, but the horse tried to get rid of the smart of it by frantically shaking his head and rubbing his nose in the dirt and against his knee.

One hour later, his muzzle was out like a balloon. The swelling moved upward toward his eyes and, before long, he could barely open them. He and the bay moved aimlessly across the valley. The other colt was not sure what had happened, but he did know the gray was in trouble. They stood together beneath an overhang of ledge. The snake venom slowly spread through Cloud's body. Sweat broke out along his neck and flanks. Chills shook his frame so hard his knees turned rubbery and threatened to collapse. This went on all night long. Daybreak found him still on his feet but terribly thirsty. He staggered to a nearby stream, but his swollen throat was unable to swallow any water.

When the swelling and fever finally left Cloud, five days later, the gray horse was hardly able to walk. He had grown thin from not eating. His flanks were drawn up and his hip bones protruded. The snake bite had drained his strength to such a degree that the effort of grazing and drinking tired him quickly, and he would lie down frequently to rest. When he did, the bay never left his side. The mornings were cooler now and the nights became quite cold. This kind of weather stimulated the mustang's circulation and his recovery from the snake bite.

The young horses ate continuously, instinctively aware that soon the snow would fly and food would be scarce. They moved across the valley with their muzzles chomping away like a pair of lawn mowers. They found ice along the water's edge in the morning and at night the bare trees trembled before a shivering wind.

Again winter rushed in from the north, cracking a chill whip and dragging a bulky robe of white over everything. But their sheltered valley was a safe haven for the two young horses, somehow protected from the outside world. They lost considerable weight, but they were fit. They became a devoted team and warded off their enemies by standing close together, nose to nose, hindquarters facing outward, to meet any attack.

One icy moonlit night, two wolves spotted the pair digging for food along the stream. The predators were hungry and moved in to try to pull one animal down before the other had a chance to come to its aid.

As the wolves charged, Cloud met them with a lightning-like kick of his hind legs that sent one wolf twenty feet up into the

air, turning over and over and all spread out like a flying squirrel. When he hit the snow, he was still running in high gear, but in the opposite direction. His fellow conspirator, in the face of Cloud's flashing counterattack, speedily joined his companion to seek easier game elsewhere.

The wind had shaped a high bank of snow in front of the cave where the two young mustangs had met, concealing it cleverly against the cliff wall. When the weather really became inclement, the pair sought refuge here, where it was cozy and dry. They temporarily changed their eating habits to become browsers, chewing on whatever brush they could dig out of the drifts and the fine branches of trees that hung low enough for them to reach. They had the company of many deer and elk. A pair of mountain lions culled the deer herd, and in February the few wolves in the area got their share, too.

March came and went uneventfully. Here in this valley, there existed a true balance of nature without any outside interference. But one day, if Cloud had not interfered, he might have lost his companion.

The gray mustang was alone that afternoon, pawing through some brush and snow, when, all at once a squeal of terror spooked him almost three feet off the ground. He came down stiff-legged as the bay came into view, floundering through a heavy drift of snow with a huge mountain lion draped across his back. The cougar was clawing for a grip on the mustang's nose so that he could jerk his head around to break the animal's neck. The snow was too deep to give the frantic horse enough solid purchase to buck off his assailant and it looked as if the big cat would make his kill.

Cloud plunged to the rescue. He collided with the lion over the top of the bay horse. The momentum of his rush sent all three rolling along the ground in a swirl of white. The lion came out of it first, spitting with frustration. Cloud went after him with striking forefeet. His teeth clicked together like a steel trap, chopping off the hairs on the tip of the lion's tail. The cat went high tailing through the deep snow, yowling each time he heard the snap of the mustang's jaws. The lion had been practically tasting his next meal and here he was, only five seconds later, trying to get away from it as fast as his churning legs would allow.

Cloud chased him clear across the white meadow. The cat finally took refuge on the lower branches of a blue spruce tree, where he lay for the remainder of the afternoon, nursing his ruffled pride.

There were no more close calls for the two horses that month. In April, large patches of brown turf appeared on the slopes which caught most of the sun's rays. A haze of green spread through the brown, which gradually deepened into new shoots of grass as the snow melted off. Then spring was suddenly upon them and by the middle of May the horses were sleek and sassy once more.

All through the following summer the local wildlife thrived. The two mustangs had no more trouble with lions or wolves but, in early July of that year, something happened which altered their way of life.

They were grazing along a narrow glen that reached up out of the valley floor and ended on top of a flat plateau. It was cool here and the horses spent the middle of the day in the shade of the jackpines that had rooted themselves on the sloping sides of the ravine. Great boulders protruded from the earth and numerous windfalls caused the horses to step slowly. Normally, they would have smelled the bear but the wind was

wrong. The lone grizzly was unaware of their approach—for he was intent on his meal of venison. The huge beast was making small whining sounds as he ripped into the red flesh of the doe which he had killed only a half hour ago. His great head came up when he heard a pebble roll. Blood dripped from the corners of his jaws. His tongue flicked out to lick them clean as his piglike eyes focused on the pair of mustangs when they came into view. The bear had had a tough day. Making this kill had taken much patience and shortened his temper to hair-trigger readiness. The sight of the intruders jerked him to his feet with a snarl of rage. He came hurtling down the draw with such speed that Cloud and the bay almost did not get out of his way in time. Because the horses shied in opposite directions, the charging bear braked to a halt for a split second, unable to decide which one to follow. Neither mustang waited around long enough to find out.

The grizzly rose to his hind legs. His wet black nose twitched as he tested the air. His temper cooled quickly and he dropped to all fours again and drank for a long time from a tiny trickle of water that wound its way down the gulley. Evidently he had eaten his fill, for he did not return to the slain doe. Instead, he ambled slowly up the side of the draw, to seek out a soft, comfortable spot to sleep off his meal.

The mustangs did not stop running until they reached the valley floor. A good many horses would never have entered that glen again, but Cloud was a curious individual and, toward evening, he ventured back into the ravine. The bay followed reluctantly, but alertly, ready for instant retreat. There, at the scene of the kill, stood a tiny fawn. The last rays of the sun had found their way into the gully and spotlighted the little creature in a golden shaft. The large, soft brown eyes were

fastened on Cloud as he approached. She had been here since the bear left. When her mother failed to show up she had ventured forth from hiding to find her.

The smell of blood had confused the young deer, urging her to run away, but the scent of her mother held her to this place. The mustang and the fawn sniffed noses. Who knows of the language between animals? But when Cloud turned away, the bewildered creature followed at a distance. Occasionally, the horse stopped and waited. When he did, the fawn trotted forward. The bay dropped in behind the fawn—and the trio walked slowly back to the valley floor.

The baby had been nursing still but circumstances weaned

her in a hurry. She browsed like a deer but mimicked the horses as they grazed. She had formed an instant attachment to Cloud and rarely left his side. In a way, she hampered the gray mustang's freedom, but he seemed to take on his new responsibility happily. He kept an eye on the baby wherever she went and always moved slowly enough for her to keep up. The bay also accepted the new addition.

When the mustangs lay down to rest, the fawn curled up between them. She had nothing to fear from predators, for it would take a brave one to storm the fortification the horses provided for their charge.

The summer passed, and when the snow blew into the valley once more the young deer was more than half grown. Her spots had disappeared and she was well on her way to maturity. Her reddish-brown summer color became a deep warm gray, with the brown showing through. Now she could keep up with the horses with not too much effort, using a peculiar running gait, a progression of stiff-legged leaps, in which the feet came down together to the ground, then bounded off again like steel springs.

The three spent a good winter together—not once were they molested by predators. As spring crept in, the doe seemed restless, sometimes standing a short distance away from the mustangs, staring up the craggy slopes as if she expected someone—as if she were listening for a sound neither horse could detect. Sometimes she wandered off at night, but always returned before daybreak.

Once Cloud caught sight of four mule deer standing quietly on a high bluff, looking down at them. Then one morning the doe did not return. Usually, the mustangs ranged over their entire valley but they stayed where they were for three days. On the fourth day, a group of deer appeared. Cloud trotted forward to investigate. The deer held their ground at first, but moved off as the gray mustang approached. Only one doe waited for him.

The horse and deer stood quietly together, nose to nose. Finally, she turned and bounded off to overtake her companions. Cloud watched them until they disappeared in a grove of cottonwood. He nickered softly, then swung back to the bay, standing behind him.

The two mustangs were alone again. This year, Cloud's winter coat had shed out to a glistening dappled pale steel color. His dark mane, forever in motion, hung to his shoulders, and his high arched tail could almost reach his forelegs when it swatted at the spring insects. His companion had become a shiny blood bay, lighter built than Cloud and nearly as beautiful.

Cloud was still the instinctive leader, the bay a natural follower. Therefore, there were no conflicts in their personalities and they were happy together in this land of plenty.

But the outside world also had been changing. Men were no longer hunting wild horses only to ride. Now they were catching them to be sent to slaughterhouses, to be used for dog or cat food. But, worst of all, their methods of capture had become "modernized." Trucks were being used that rolled across the ground at high speed—much faster than any horse could run. There were also airplanes that dropped out of the sky to pursue the frantic animals from above.

In their lovely valley, Cloud and the bay had found a horse paradise, with no premonition of the invasion which had already begun.

6

THE day was hot—and the two young horses walking listlessly across the barren flat were hot, too. They had been on the move since dawn. They were restless and disturbed. There was a troubled feeling in the still air which kept whispering, "Watch out! Watch out!" Had they been a part of the band, they would have been warned by the stallion leader that danger lurked everywhere. But they were both young and inexperienced. They had grown up almost without parental supervision and, as a result, were unprepared for what lay ahead.

Right now, they were terribly thirsty. Neither had had any water since they had left Cloud's favorite valley, and that was over seven hours ago. The summer had been abnormally hot, with little rain. All the watering stations they passed were dry and even the creek beds were cracking up under the blistering sun. But the horses kept moving forward in slow motion, as if in a dream, too thirsty to stop and almost too tired to go on.

A breeze came up from the south and crept sluggishly across the parched land. As it passed over Cloud and the bay, their heads suddenly lifted and their nostrils dilated—water! The scent of water! They broke into a trot, then simultaneously rolled into a ground-eating gallop. The terrain dipped steeply toward a grove of scattered trees and brush. There was water in there —but there was also another smell in the air that should have stopped them.

A cowboy, lying along a branch of a tree near the water hole, watched them approach.

"Hey, Mike," he whispered down to his partner, who was leaning against the tree trunk, "there are two of them heading this way right now. You'd better duck out of sight before they get here—and tell Luke to mount up."

This was the only water hole within twenty miles. The men had been working for three days, constructing a trap around it. Using logs and brush and wire, they had built a well-camouflaged enclosure more than 160 feet in diameter. It was almost nine feet tall and, they figured, strong enough to hold an elephant. The man lying on the overhanging branch braced himself, waiting to drop the gate the second the horses moved inside.

Cloud entered the trap three bounds in front of the bay colt, then jumped twenty feet ahead when the closing gate slammed to the earth behind the pair. The gray whirled and froze—and instantly whirled again. He could see nothing unusual and, as yet, he had not detected his enemy. It never occurred to him that he was trapped. But he sensed that there was something wrong. The bay horse crowded against him. He, too, was completely perplexed by what had happened, but he looked to Cloud to make the next move. Five seconds ticked by. A voice from somewhere shouted, "We got 'em, Luke!"

Cloud had heard that fearful outcry before. Like a bolt of

lightning, the memories of his early years descended upon the gray colt, urging him into a swirling blaze of action that sent him around the enclosure three times, rapidly exploring every opening. He stopped abruptly when he realized he was locked in. As the dust settled, he could see his bay companion still standing where he had left him. But Cloud had too much of his gray sire in him to give up so easily.

There had to be a way out! Of course there was—the same way he had come in! His thirst was forgotten now. He approached the gate cautiously, sizing it up. When he had decided what to do, he broke into a trot, then, two strides before the barrier, he set himself and, with a tremendous impulsion, leaped toward the top bars. He hung over them for a fraction of a second, then seemed to gather himself again in midair. The rails rattled as he skimmed across them. The baked earth on the outside rose to meet him and, even as he landed, his hindquarters came in under him and he was off. For the next two hundred yards he flew as if he had been shot out of a cannon, then, abruptly, came to a sliding halt when he heard the bay cry out behind him. Spinning about, he whinnied shrilly, frantically. The bay answered in panic but he was still frozen where Cloud had left him, inside the trap. The gray colt went galloping back, but he was much more alert now. So far, he had seen no sign of human enemies but he knew they were there. When he reached the gate, he met the bay nose to nose through the bars. He could not leave him behind! He began circling the enclosure, the bay keeping pace with him on the inside.

Suddenly, without warning, Cloud came face to face with a strange horse. There was a man on his back, twirling a rope. For a heartbeat there was no sound save the swishing hum of the lariat. It all happened so fast and unexpectedly that Cloud

had barely enough time to duck sideways when the loop whirled past. Two more riders appeared, blocking his escape to the left, so he broke away to the right, racing close to the boulder-strewn base of the steep wall above the water hole. In the next instant, the three men were spurring after him, all swinging ropes about their heads.

Cloud quickly outdistanced them, but they kept up the chase and presently cornered him. Again he broke away, dodged a flying rope, then flung himself at a rock slide, in a valiant attempt to scale it. While he fought upward in the slipping shale, the horsemen converged behind him.

A quick noose leaped forward and settled over the gray colt's ears. A rider whirled and rode away, his horse leaning against the pull of the lariat tied to the saddle horn. Unbalanced, Cloud leaped, turned in midair like a cat, and slid down the shale to the valley floor. Here, for a long instant, he was a great vibrant picture of savage defiance, his head up and his eyes blazing. Then he charged, low and fast.

The other two riders snaked their ropes forward and down, trying for his feet. He was too quick for them, though. The man on the rope horse flung himself to one side, but Cloud's striking forefeet caught him and hurled him clear out of the saddle. His horse was bowled over by the charge. The gray colt ran on, headed for freedom, but the rope, still tied to the saddle horn of the downed horse, whipped taut and spun him about. Then Cloud went mad. Cold, savage fury surged through him. With a shrill cry of rage, he rushed at the man on the ground, his teeth bared viciously.

At that instant, a loop came spinning out of nowhere and snapped tightly around the gray's front legs. He went down as if he had been clubbed.

He struck the earth so hard it exploded under him, sending out geysers of dust in all directions. He lay there, stunned. Before he could recover, a man was sitting on his head and, in spite of his frantic kicks, the gray was unable to dislodge him. Five seconds later, a heavy rope halter was slipped over his head. Then he was allowed to scramble to his feet once more. He stood spraddle legged and trembling. The rope quivered in front of his eyes. His gaze followed along it to a man on a horse. He must get away from here. He made another wild dash, only to be jerked up short by pressure on his nose. After a few minutes, the man turned his pony, trying to get the gray colt to follow, but the captive squatted back on his haunches, shaking his head and bracing his forelegs against the steady pull. One of the cowboys laid a quirt sharply across his rump, causing the wild horse to shoot forward. This was his first lesson in leading. The rope must be obeyed, and there was no use struggling against it.

After Cloud was snubbed to a stout tree, the three men departed. About fifty feet away, he could see the bay, snubbed to another tree. At least, he was not completely alone. But he was exhausted. Sweat rolled down his flanks and dripped from his belly. The long day, the heat, the thirst, the chase had finally knocked the fight out of him.

The following morning, two of the mounted cowboys returned to work with Cloud and the bay, taking the ropes and leading them about. Neither mustang gave the men any trouble. Evidently, Cloud had decided to play it their way, and the bay seemed willing enough to follow suit. This went on for the rest of the day. That night, the pair was turned loose with the pack and saddle horses, to graze in the fenced-in waterhole.

The domestic stock eyed the mustangs suspiciously. They milled about for a bit with ears flattened, but in a little while all settled down to eat. The trap gate had another pole added to its height, to discourage Cloud from further attempts to escape.

The next morning, the two wild horses were caught and tied to trees again. One man stayed at the campsite, up behind the trap. The other two mustangers, Mike and Luke, worked around them and with them, teaching them that a halter was something to be tolerated and that it was useless to fight the pull of a rope. Before long, the captives reached the point where, even though still suspicious, they stopped fighting the rope and began to lead readily.

One morning, the three horsemen, driving their pack animals before them and leading the two young mustangs, rode through the open trap gate and out into the mesa. Perhaps getting into the open country again reminded Cloud and the bay of the wild band to which they had belonged long ago, for, several times, they neighed shrilly and lunged at their ropes.

The riders headed westward and traveled all day in that direction with their captured horses. The blowing wind was rich with the smell of juniper and sage. That night, the wild mustangs were watered at a cold spring, then tied in a grove of willows, where they could feed on the tender limb tips. The riding and pack horses were turned loose to graze.

The trail to which the men held was vaguely familiar to Cloud. When he saw the river, it all came back in a rush—this was where he had lived with the wild bunch during that first winter of his life. They had not gone farther than the river then. Their gray leader had known that barbed wire and civilization lay beyond. But this time, Cloud and his bay companion forded the river and, before long, were on a dirt road. Barbed-wire fences lined both sides and, occasionally, the mustangs saw strange structures with white-faced cattle and tame horses feeding peacefully nearby. Dogs barked and yapped as they went by and, once or twice, the group passed other men mounted on horses, going in the opposite direction. A small pickup truck came chugging along and the cowboys had all they could do to keep the two wild horses on the ground. But it passed without harming anyone and the next time one went by the two horses tensed up but managed to keep cool.

As the cavalcade jogged along, the ranches became more numerous. Once they were held up at a railroad crossing. When an enormous, sputtering locomotive arrived, with much rattling noise and a sickening odor, Cloud and the bay bolted. They galloped down the road the way they had come, dragging the mounted cowboys behind them and scattering the pack animals before them. They all pulled up almost a mile away. It took more than an hour and a good deal of coaxing to get the outfit rounded up, on course again, and over the glistening twin tracks of the crossing.

That night, Cloud and the bay were turned into a high pole corral. Both horses diligently examined every crack and corner before they turned their attention to eating for the first time the unfamiliar new, fresh hay that had been thrown in for them.

The mustangers met with two strange men. They talked softly for a long time. Then there was much laughing, money was exchanged, and the mustangers rode off. The new owners of the wild horses sat around a fire for awhile. Finally, they wrapped themselves in blankets and slept.

Early the next morning, the captive pair was driven by their new owners into a long chute, up a dirt ramp, and onto the bed of a large truck with high sides and a canvas cover overhead. There were several other captured mustangs aboard and they crowded away from the newcomers. For a moment, it seemed as if a kicking contest was about to begin, but, when the vehicle jolted into motion, the animals had all they could do to keep from falling down.

All day long they traveled eastward. Through the parallel slats, Cloud could see the countryside slide swiftly by. Thousands of odd and unknown odors rushed through his prison as the truck sped away from the sunset. Most of the time, the ride was fairly smooth but, occasionally, the horses were hurled from

side to side by deeply rutted dirt roads.

That night, the truck stopped on the outskirts of a small town, just north of Cheyenne, Wyoming. The wild mustangs were unloaded and hazed into a large corral in which there were a great many more horses. The long, hard ride had taken much of the fight out of them. Now they endured their confinement meekly, with their heads down, staring listlessly at the bare, hard-packed earth. Only Cloud moved quietly around his enclosure, investigating every loose rail and opening. Later, he stood beside the bay, with his head up, his muzzle searching the breeze that lifted his forelock as it drifted across the backs of the dozing captives. Apprehension had left the gray. Now there was a strange calm about him, as a new kind of strength, perhaps the heritage of his fiery ancestors, began coursing through his veins. Like his sire, it was not his nature to give up. At last, he accepted the fact that his initial battle for freedom was lost—but the war was not over yet!

7

CLOUD expected to be taken out again the following morning but it was almost noon before several cowboys appeared. The early part of the day had been quite cool but now it was beginning to warm up. He stood apart from the other mustangs, seemingly relaxed and at ease, but an observer who knew anything about horses could have seen that the gray colt was sharply alert, studying every move of the men who were sizing up the animals.

"That's about the best bunch of wild horses I ever did see," one man declared. "There's some hot blood in that gray." He hooked his thumb toward Cloud.

"I'll bet he's got a real good buck in him," another ventured.

If Cloud did have "a real good buck," it would be a stroke of luck, for most of these horses were headed for some dog meat packing companies in the East. One or two might make saddle horses—and perhaps the same number would be picked for the rodeo arena.

After some discussion, it was decided to "buck 'em out."

Cloud kept a wary eye on one of the cowboys as he hazed a big, rawboned black into a narrow, high-walled box. The gate was fastened shut and a saddle was quickly dropped down and snugly cinched up. The frightened horse tried to fight it but there was hardly enough room in the chute to turn his head. Before the animal knew what was happening, a rider slipped into the saddle and the box gate swung open. For one instant, the black didn't budge, then, suddenly, he dropped his head, came out sideways, and went bucking along the corral fence. Abruptly, he changed direction with a twisting snap that sent his rider flying.

"He's a good one!" The man laughed as he rolled to his feet and began beating the dust out of his blue jeans.

Two more horses were tried out, including the bay, who only crowhopped a bit and began running around the enclosure.

"He'll make someone a fine cowpony," shouted one man approvingly. As they led his companion from the corral, Cloud nickered and trotted in his direction.

"Get that one," roared one of the bystanders. A lariat dropped over Cloud's head. The bay was forgotten. Cloud accepted the chute as if he'd been in one before. Everyone stopped talking while the saddle was cinched into place. The gray's quiet attitude lulled his rider into a false sense of security. Most broncs had given him some indication of what lay ahead, but this one did not quiver a muscle. The cowboy reached for the halter shank and shouted, "Let 'er rip!" and the gate swung wide.

Afterward, nobody could say for sure what happened next. In one jump, Cloud was air borne. It was not a straight buck, for on the top of his arch he swapped ends, then hit the earth like a pile driver. The best of riders could not have sat out that one and this rider was no exception. He climbed to his

feet, shaking his head and wiping the blood from his mouth with the back of his hand. "Beats me, beats me," he kept saying over and over. Everyone was shouting at once.

"He's the best I've ever seen," cried Max Linder, the man who had bought the truckload of wild horses. "Now there is a horse! He's a born fighter—a natural. I'll make a real bucking bronc out of this one. You wait and see. A good bucking horse

is worth a heck of a lot more than a good saddle horse these days." He slapped his hat joyously against his thigh. "Hell's fire, man, I'm gonna train him to be the best in the rodeo business. Yes, sir, that ol' bronc will make a lot of money for me!"

If the gray horse had understood what this man was saying, he might have answered, "That's what you think!"

Cloud's education as a bucking horse outlaw began immediately, and the man Linder was a capable teacher. He had a devilish understanding of horse nature, knowing just how to infuriate the animal in order to arouse him to a wild state of frantic desperation. Men got on Cloud's back, men with cruel, raking spurs and sharp quirts, and, when the chute gate swung open, the gray grew to expect a cut on the flanks and rowels jammed into his shoulders. He reacted in the only way he could, bucking, lunging, twisting, fighting. He didn't know how to quit. He *was* a born fighter. When he exploded into the open, he came all unhinged, striking in ten directions at once, with a viciousness that was terrifying to watch and practically impossible to sit on. And he didn't stop bucking until the weight was gone from the saddle and the halter rein was dangling loose.

Linder watched the development of his prize bucker from the safety of the top rail of the corral. He had been a bronc rider himself when he was younger and less cautious. "The only advantage in getting older is getting smarter," he told anyone who cared to listen. These days, he hired young, foolhardy men to do his dirty work.

Daily, for a period of several weeks, the gray was run into the chute and turned out with either a man in the saddle or a dummy tied on in such a fashion that it would come loose after a few jumps. Linder prepared Cloud for the rodeo arena as a fight manager prepares his fighter for the ring. "Let him win again and again until he feels he's invincible and unbeatable," was Linder's slogan. They gray learned to go high on that first jump and come back to earth with a jarring, stiff-legged jolt. He learned to spin, and leap, and turn his belly to the sun, then twist like a cat in midair and land rightside up, ready to blast off again.

Linder happily watched the mustang's progress and, the meaner the gray became, the broader grew the smile on his swarthy face.

During this period of training, Cloud became accustomed to the corral, to living in close quarters with other horses—fellow gladiators also being prepared for the rodeo arena. Since the loss of his bay companion, he had made no attachments, to man or beast. He had learned that it was useless to rebel against the chute, that nothing could be gained by fighting the saddle and cinch. He saved his strength for the instant the gate opened—it was the only freedom he had enjoyed since his capture. Linder gave him little time to remember his unrestricted past, but Cloud never forgot it. So far, though, no opportunity for escape had presented itself to him. In recent weeks he had developed a new kind of patience, deadly and unforgiving. His time would come—and when it did, he would be ready.

8

THIS intensive course in making bucking horses out of wild mustangs continued until one afternoon, when a large number of horsemen gathered about the corral and a noisy crowd of people filled the grandstand. A brass band blared forth loud, hideous noises, and from somewhere above, a gruff voice announced over a loudspeaker that the rodeo was about to begin.

The wild horses milled nervously in their pen. This was something they had never before experienced. The big, raw-boned black was cut out first and hazed into the bucking chute. He fought and reared as the saddle was buckled down and his rider slid into position. He blew into the arena like a horse gone crazy. It took three twisting bucks to loosen his rider—the third sent him spread-eagled into the dust.

Two more broncs went out before Cloud. The qualifying time was ten seconds in the saddle—both of their riders made it.

The cowboy who drew the gray mustang lasted only one jump. The wild horse leaped straight up out of the chute gate and came straight down on his front legs, so perpendicular to the ground it seemed, for an instant, that he might go over on his back. He did not, but the rider did, the impact of his fall knocking the wind right out of him. As Cloud galloped back to the corral gate beside the pickup man, the crowd leaped to its feet and roared with approval. They had just witnessed a top-notch bucker in action and they knew it.

Linder couldn't have been more pleased. "He'll make the big time," he proudly declared. "He's a cyclone—a natural bucking horse."

But Linder was wrong. Cloud was not a natural bucking horse. He was a natural fighter, with a marvelous instinct for self-preservation and survival. He had an uncanny ability for self-discipline, saving his strength, then mustering his forces for one all-out tremendous effort when it was really needed. As a yearling, he had done the impossible, climbing the steep cliff wall to escape the mustangers, then, later, leaping over the trap gate under similar desperate circumstances.

Now, as a rodeo bronc, he was instinctively making the best of a bad situation. He didn't waste his energy battling against his captors but bided his time—saving himself for the opening which, sooner or later, was bound to present itself.

The rodeo continued for three days. Cloud went out three times. Nobody rode him for more than five seconds. Then, for two days, the bucking stock was permitted to rest.

On the third evening, they were led into large vans and tied ear to tail. There were three vans in all, each carrying twenty horses. When the floor began rocking under them, most of the horses swayed and snorted in alarm. But Cloud had vanned before and, because he learned quickly, he just braced his legs and barely moved for the rest of the journey.

They traveled all night long and, in the morning, came to a

with it. Only the halter rope swung from his head.

While he galloped across the arena, the gray could see men in yellow slickers rushing for cover, to escape the deluge from above. Suddenly, he realized he was alone—even the pickup man was nowhere to be seen. All this happened in seconds, and it took Cloud just about that time to make up his mind. His moment for escape had come!

One turn around the arena gave him his bearings. A five-foot gate closed one narrow end of the stadium and that was the direction he took, running flat out, with his head held low against the storm. He met the gate in stride—soared up and over with ease. A parked convertible blocked his way. He jumped again —and he was clear. On he ran, through the alley, between the cattlepens, then out onto a hard-top road.

Most of the people were huddled in doorways, out of the storm. The few hurrying along the streets stopped and stared as the gray mustang went flying by. Instinctively, he turned northwest. He did not know why, except that somewhere in the re-
esses of his memory, he saw a river out there, with purple hills
sing beyond. A policeman leaped to the middle of the road,
aving his arms in an effort to slow down the running horse.
Cloud skirted around him, the man reached out and caught
halter shank. But there wasn't a chance in the world that he
ld stop the frightened mustang. He let go after two strides,
ng to the slippery pavement. The rain was easing up now.
d of the fleeing horse loomed a tie-up of traffic, with many
hiny automobiles and honking horns. Cloud zigzagged be-
the cars like a broken-field runner, hardly missing a stride.
dy else tried to interfere with his progress.
e crossed the village green, his flashing hoofs ripped up
lumps of turf. Beyond the green, the road shot straight

halt near a group of corrals. These were bigger than the ones they had vacated yesterday. This set-up also had two more chutes and a much larger grandstand.

The wild horses were put into a spacious corral behind the arena. The other pens held calves and cattle of every description, for this rodeo included other events besides bucking contests—calf roping, steer wrestling and bull riding.

The show lasted four days—and, in that time, Cloud worked approximately nine seconds and eight jumps to throw his four riders.

For the remainder of the summer, Cloud and the other mustangs were moved from one rodeo arena to the next. The gray's reputation as a bucking bronc grew. As in the days of the early West, when one top gunfighter was challenged by other gunfighters, to prove who was the best man, so Cloud was challenged by the top bronc riders in the area. So far, not one was able to qualify on him for the required ten-second ride.

Early in September, Linder and his bucking string headed for the Sky High Frontier Days, one of the great rodeos of the West. The contestants came from all over the United States and Canada, to prove themselves. The best in the business met here —the best riders, the best ropers, the best bulldoggers, and the toughest bucking broncs—for to be a "top gun" here was one of the highest achievements in the rodeo world.

Linder's horses arrived at night and were quickly and quietly unloaded at the corrals. There was a network of these that formed a semicircle behind the arena. Two large grandstands faced one another on the long sides of the stadium. The steeply sloped roofs had many gaily colored flags fluttering along their crests.

Before the contest began, numbers were drawn by the riders to determine the horses to be ridden each day—the show was scheduled to run a full week.

Cloud was calm. By this time, he knew the ropes pretty well. He knew his job and how to perform it as quickly and as efficiently as possible.

The morning of the first day of the rodeo dawned clear, even though thunderstorms were predicted. But around one o'clock in the afternoon, dark, ominous clouds appeared on the western horizon and began moving swiftly eastward. A wind came up. Large swirls of dust and parts of newspapers began whipping across the earth. The saddle-bronc riding competitions were just starting. The broncs were hazed through a wood-framed alleyway and into the line of bucking chutes located along the eastern side of the arena. Streaks of lightning were lancing across the heavens, making the horses more edgy than usual.

Cloud stood in Chute No. 4, waiting to be called. His halter was in place and his saddle was cinched down. Only the flank strap hung loosely, to be pulled up tight when the chute gate opened. Thunder rolled in the distance.

The first contestant was announced over the loud-speaker. It was an eight-second ride. The next man stayed on his mount the full ten. The third rider also went all the way. The rain began coming down.

Then a voice boomed over the loud-speaker, "Out of Chute No. 4, Max Linder's all-time great bucking horse, Blue Cyclone, with Bud Slocum aboard."

The rider was in the saddle now, halter shank in his left hand, feet braced forward against the wooden stirrups. "Let's go!" he called to the gate man.

Just as Cloud exploded into the ring, there was a great crash of thunder. The heavens opened and the water roared down ward as the gray horse rose to meet it. He rolled in midair, b when he touched the soaked earth once more, his legs shot ways and the impact of his 1,200 pounds sent the mud out under him like a huge brown fountain. The rider was th clear but, as Cloud lunged to his feet, the cinch burst loo the saddle slid back off his hindquarters, taking the fla

ahead, between white picket fences and trim lawns and a row of development houses. Cloud looked neither to right nor left. In the distance, he could see fields and mountains sweeping upward. They drew him like a magnet. Now he was galloping alongside a barbed-wire fence, looking for a way inland. He found it—a cattle guard across an open gateway. He jumped it. When his feet met the grassy turf on the other side, he shifted into high gear once more, still pointed northwest, toward those beckoning hills.

9

CLOUD loped along until sunset. He was pretty tired by then, for he was out of condition from being penned up for so long. He stopped only once—to rid himself of the halter. Catching the cheek strap against a post, he pulled backward until the headpiece slipped over his ears. He was released from the last remnant of civilization.

Cloud spent that night grazing with a small bunch of cattle in the moonlight and, for the first time in many days, he knew peace.

Morning found him moving northwest once more. The blood was surging in his veins. He was free again, free, free! His eyes were lifted to the foothills ahead, coming closer and closer. He saw small towns and villages—and bypassed them all. Men lived there—and men were those loathsome creatures of whom he wanted no part ever again.

After having spent so many months in the narrow confines of rodeo corrals, the gray reveled in the wild freedom of the mesas, and he quickly fell back into the old routine of life. He fed on the luscious grass in the coolness of the early morning, and rested in the shade of willow and aspen thickets during the midday heat. But he never lost track of the direction in which he was going. He mingled with cows frequently. He found them good companions, and they never seemed to mind his presence.

One afternoon, Cloud ran into two cowboys, who immediately gave chase. They were well mounted and came on faster than he expected. Two miles rolled by with the gray mustang keeping up an easy lope. Then, as he topped a ridge, a barbed-wire fence blocked his way. Ordinarily, he would have tried to skirt it. Barbed wire was to be avoided at all costs. But this fence had large tufts of animal hairs hanging from the top strand, where cattle had been scratching their backs. It made the wire clearly visible against the sky, enabling him to measure its height from the ground and leap it with the grace of a jumping deer.

The cowboys pulled up, cursing their bad luck. It was just as well that the barbed wire had cut off their pursuit, for they never could have caught up with the gray stallion, anyway.

The fifth day after Cloud had escaped from the rodeo arena, as he crested a long rise, he saw a river below. He came down to it cautiously. Evidently, there had been much rain in the hills, for the yellow rushing water made a rumbling noise. Logs and branches of trees rose up out of the white foam on the surface, like strange fish leaping for flies. The mustang moved upstream, searching in vain for a ford where he might cross. He proceeded slowly along the shore, occasionally stepping out into the hissing current but pulling back quickly when the cold water splashed against his belly.

As he hesitated there, undecided, a painfully familiar scent touched his nostrils, causing him to wheel away from the river,

the ground it seemed, for an instant, that he might go over on his back. He did not, but the rider did, the impact of his fall knocking the wind right out of him. As Cloud galloped back to the corral gate beside the pickup man, the crowd leaped to its feet and roared with approval. They had just witnessed a top-notch bucker in action and they knew it.

Linder couldn't have been more pleased. "He'll make the big time," he proudly declared. "He's a cyclone—a natural bucking horse."

But Linder was wrong. Cloud was not a natural bucking horse. He was a natural fighter, with a marvelous instinct for self-preservation and survival. He had an uncanny ability for self-discipline, saving his strength, then mustering his forces for one all-out tremendous effort when it was really needed. As a yearling, he had done the impossible, climbing the steep cliff wall to escape the mustangers, then, later, leaping over the trap gate under similar desperate circumstances.

Now, as a rodeo bronc, he was instinctively making the best of a bad situation. He didn't waste his energy battling against his captors but bided his time—saving himself for the opening which, sooner or later, was bound to present itself.

The rodeo continued for three days. Cloud went out three times. Nobody rode him for more than five seconds. Then, for two days, the bucking stock was permitted to rest.

On the third evening, they were led into large vans and tied ear to tail. There were three vans in all, each carrying twenty horses. When the floor began rocking under them, most of the horses swayed and snorted in alarm. But Cloud had vanned before and, because he learned quickly, he just braced his legs and barely moved for the rest of the journey.

They traveled all night long and, in the morning, came to a

8

THIS intensive course in making bucking horses out of wild mustangs continued until one afternoon, when a large number of horsemen gathered about the corral and a noisy crowd of people filled the grandstand. A brass band blared forth loud, hideous noises, and from somewhere above, a gruff voice announced over a loudspeaker that the rodeo was about to begin.

The wild horses milled nervously in their pen. This was something they had never before experienced. The big, rawboned black was cut out first and hazed into the bucking chute. He fought and reared as the saddle was buckled down and his rider slid into position. He blew into the arena like a horse gone crazy. It took three twisting bucks to loosen his rider—the third sent him spread-eagled into the dust.

Two more broncs went out before Cloud. The qualifying time was ten seconds in the saddle—both of their riders made it.

The cowboy who drew the gray mustang lasted only one jump. The wild horse leaped straight up out of the chute gate and came straight down on his front legs, so perpendicular to halt near a group of corrals. These were bigger than the ones they had vacated yesterday. This set-up also had two more chutes and a much larger grandstand.

The wild horses were put into a spacious corral behind the arena. The other pens held calves and cattle of every description, for this rodeo included other events besides bucking contests—calf roping, steer wrestling and bull riding.

The show lasted four days—and, in that time, Cloud worked approximately nine seconds and eight jumps to throw his four riders.

For the remainder of the summer, Cloud and the other mustangs were moved from one rodeo arena to the next. The gray's reputation as a bucking bronc grew. As in the days of the early West, when one top gunfighter was challenged by other gunfighters, to prove who was the best man, so Cloud was challenged by the top bronc riders in the area. So far, not one was able to qualify on him for the required ten-second ride.

Early in September, Linder and his bucking string headed for the Sky High Frontier Days, one of the great rodeos of the West. The contestants came from all over the United States and Canada, to prove themselves. The best in the business met here—the best riders, the best ropers, the best bulldoggers, and the toughest bucking broncs—for to be a "top gun" here was one of the highest achievements in the rodeo world.

Linder's horses arrived at night and were quickly and quietly unloaded at the corrals. There was a network of these that formed a semicircle behind the arena. Two large grandstands faced one another on the long sides of the stadium. The steeply sloped roofs had many gaily colored flags fluttering along their crests.

Before the contest began, numbers were drawn by the riders to determine the horses to be ridden each day—the show was scheduled to run a full week.

Cloud was calm. By this time, he knew the ropes pretty well. He knew his job and how to perform it as quickly and as efficiently as possible.

The morning of the first day of the rodeo dawned clear, even though thunderstorms were predicted. But around one o'clock in the afternoon, dark, ominous clouds appeared on the western horizon and began moving swiftly eastward. A wind came up. Large swirls of dust and parts of newspapers began whipping across the earth. The saddle-bronc riding competitions were just starting. The broncs were hazed through a wood-framed alleyway and into the line of bucking chutes located along the eastern side of the arena. Streaks of lightning were lancing across the heavens, making the horses more edgy than usual.

Cloud stood in Chute No. 4, waiting to be called. His halter was in place and his saddle was cinched down. Only the flank strap hung loosely, to be pulled up tight when the chute gate opened. Thunder rolled in the distance.

The first contestant was announced over the loud-speaker. It was an eight-second ride. The next man stayed on his mount the full ten. The third rider also went all the way. The rain began coming down.

Then a voice boomed over the loud-speaker, "Out of Chute No. 4, Max Linder's all-time great bucking horse, Blue Cyclone, with Bud Slocum aboard."

The rider was in the saddle now, halter shank in his left hand, feet braced forward against the wooden stirrups. "Let's go!" he called to the gate man.

Just as Cloud exploded into the ring, there was a great crash of thunder. The heavens opened and the water roared downward as the gray horse rose to meet it. He rolled in midair, but when he touched the soaked earth once more, his legs shot side ways and the impact of his 1,200 pounds sent the mud out from under him like a huge brown fountain. The rider was thrown clear but, as Cloud lunged to his feet, the cinch burst loose and the saddle slid back off his hindquarters, taking the flank strap with it. Only the halter rope swung from his head.

While he galloped across the arena, the gray could see men in yellow slickers rushing for cover, to escape the deluge from above. Suddenly, he realized he was alone—even the pickup man was nowhere to be seen. All this happened in seconds, and it took Cloud just about that time to make up his mind. His moment for escape had come!

One turn around the arena gave him his bearings. A five-foot gate closed one narrow end of the stadium and that was the direction he took, running flat out, with his head held low against the storm. He met the gate in stride—soared up and over with ease. A parked convertible blocked his way. He jumped again —and he was clear. On he ran, through the alley, between the cattlepens, then out onto a hard-top road.

Most of the people were huddled in doorways, out of the storm. The few hurrying along the streets stopped and stared as the gray mustang went flying by. Instinctively, he turned northwest. He did not know why, except that somewhere in the recesses of his memory, he saw a river out there, with purple hills rising beyond. A policeman leaped to the middle of the road, waving his arms in an effort to slow down the running horse. As Cloud skirted around him, the man reached out and caught the halter shank. But there wasn't a chance in the world that he could stop the frightened mustang. He let go after two strides, falling to the slippery pavement. The rain was easing up now. Ahead of the fleeing horse loomed a tie-up of traffic, with many wet, shiny automobiles and honking horns. Cloud zigzagged between the cars like a broken-field runner, hardly missing a stride. Nobody else tried to interfere with his progress.

As he crossed the village green, his flashing hoofs ripped up huge clumps of turf. Beyond the green, the road shot straight

ahead, between white picket fences and trim lawns and a row of development houses. Cloud looked neither to right nor left. In the distance, he could see fields and mountains sweeping upward. They drew him like a magnet. Now he was galloping alongside a barbed-wire fence, looking for a way inland. He found it—a cattle guard across an open gateway. He jumped it. When his feet met the grassy turf on the other side, he shifted into high gear once more, still pointed northwest, toward those beckoning hills.

9

CLOUD loped along until sunset. He was pretty tired by then, for he was out of condition from being penned up for so long. He stopped only once—to rid himself of the halter. Catching the cheek strap against a post, he pulled backward until the headpiece slipped over his ears. He was released from the last remnant of civilization.

Cloud spent that night grazing with a small bunch of cattle in the moonlight and, for the first time in many days, he knew peace.

Morning found him moving northwest once more. The blood was surging in his veins. He was free again, free, free! His eyes were lifted to the foothills ahead, coming closer and closer. He saw small towns and villages—and bypassed them all. Men lived there—and men were those loathsome creatures of whom he wanted no part ever again.

After having spent so many months in the narrow confines of rodeo corrals, the gray reveled in the wild freedom of the mesas, and he quickly fell back into the old routine of life. He fed on the luscious grass in the coolness of the early morning, and rested in the shade of willow and aspen thickets during the mid-day heat. But he never lost track of the direction in which he was going. He mingled with cows frequently. He found them good companions, and they never seemed to mind his presence.

One afternoon, Cloud ran into two cowboys, who immediately gave chase. They were well mounted and came on faster than he expected. Two miles rolled by with the gray mustang keeping up an easy lope. Then, as he topped a ridge, a barbed-wire fence blocked his way. Ordinarily, he would have tried to skirt it. Barbed wire was to be avoided at all costs. But this fence had large tufts of animal hairs hanging from the top strand, where cattle had been scratching their backs. It made the wire clearly visible against the sky, enabling him to measure its height from the ground and leap it with the grace of a jumping deer.

The cowboys pulled up, cursing their bad luck. It was just as well that the barbed wire had cut off their pursuit, for they never could have caught up with the gray stallion, anyway.

The fifth day after Cloud had escaped from the rodeo arena, as he crested a long rise, he saw a river below. He came down to it cautiously. Evidently, there had been much rain in the hills, for the yellow rushing water made a rumbling noise. Logs and branches of trees rose up out of the white foam on the surface, like strange fish leaping for flies. The mustang moved upstream, searching in vain for a ford where he might cross. He proceeded slowly along the shore, occasionally stepping out into the hissing current but pulling back quickly when the cold water splashed against his belly.

As he hesitated there, undecided, a painfully familiar scent touched his nostrils, causing him to wheel away from the river,

just in time to see four horsemen bearing down upon him. They seemed to be coming silently, for the sound of the pounding hoofs of their mounts was drowned out by the roar of the river. There was no room for indecision now. Cloud spun about on his hindquarters and leaped far out into the rampaging current. He was instantly sucked under, twirled about, and spewed upward. He broke surface gasping for air, then rolled sideways as a huge log rammed against his right shoulder. He was helpless in the plunging torrent. Thrashing away like a paddle-wheel steamboat, he aimed for the far shore. Once or twice, as he spun in the undertow, he was aware of the cowboys trying to keep up with him along the shore, but he was rapidly leaving them behind. The river took a sharp turn and the pursuers were gone.

Giant boulders rose on all sides as Cloud shot between them in a maelstrom of white spray. Fighting to keep his head up, he was buffeted mercilessly by rocks, logs, branches—all manner of debris. He was beginning to weaken, but his bruised and fatigued muscles refused to give up. As he labored against his rapidly diminishing strength, the current relaxed abruptly. Off to his left, he could make out the shoreline, perhaps fifty yards away. He struggled in that direction. His legs felt as if they were loaded with lead. His neck had barely enough energy to keep his head aloft. At last, his knees struck bottom. He lurched toward the land, fell, then managed to drag himself to his feet once more. He went down again. This time, his head was cushioned on the bank, so he let himself collapse in the icy water. His breath came in convulsive gasps. His lungs were burning with exertion.

Cloud lay there for almost an hour, as if he were dead. Two buzzards, flying overhead, sighted him and dove down to sit on a dead tree beside the mustang. They were preparing to feast when the gray head lifted. Cloud lurched to his feet and the huge birds soared away. Blood oozed from the many cuts and gashes that perforated his hide. But he was alive.

Cloud found himself in a narrow gorge. Painfully, he stumbled up the rocky bank and began looking for a way out. In a little while, he came to a narrow gully that sliced through the stone wall of the canyon. Water trickled down it and the mustang picked a path along the shale-covered bottom. The stream came to the surface on a wide green meadow. Here, the sun had warmed the earth and Cloud lay down again, flat on his side, and slept until the chill night air broke into his dreams.

When he got to his feet, he was so sore he could barely walk. His cuts burned and his muscles rebelled against every move. Soon, he found what he had been looking for—a patch of wet clay, kept saturated by a cold spring which bubbled out of the hillside above it. Here he lay down and wallowed, plastering his sore, fly-tortured wounds with the soothing mud. Luxuriously, he rolled, first on one side and then on the other. His blood was circulating more normally now. He climbed slowly to his feet and began grazing.

The following morning, Cloud turned again into the hills. They were all about him now. His home range—the range of his birth—could not be too far away.

At noon, the gray met up with two young stallions, grazing alone. Evidently, they had been driven from some wild band by the stallion leader and were now on their own. Cloud stayed on with them—giving himself time for his wounds to heal and his strength to return.

Glorious, hazy Indian Summer came, granting the three mustangs a last few weeks in which to fill their bellies, put on extra layers of fat, and grow long, thick coats of hair, in preparation for the winter.

Then, one morning, the trio awoke to find big heavy flakes of snow sifting down. This was low country, so Cloud sensed he had better stay where he was for the time being. The hard winter lay ahead, when he would be pawing with bloody hoofs through icy crusts for the scant feed underneath. But he wanted nothing better.

The winter had never seemed so long. Cloud and the two other stallions stuck pretty close, for together they could ward off all predators. During one period, they were harassed by several wolves. This went on for almost a week, day and night. Each time the mustangs began digging in the snow for food, one or two wolves would rush in and try to separate them.

They almost succeeded several times, but their attack backfired when one of the wolves became separated and was trampled to death by the enraged mustangs. After that, the other wolves left the horses to hunt for more cooperative victims.

Spring found Cloud gaunt and thin but his strength was back. His wounds had healed beautifully, except for one long, thin scar down his right shoulder. Now he was ready once more to find his own band. He turned purposefully northwest again. The two young horses trailed behind him.

Cloud was four years old now, approaching maturity. His frame had filled out again. His rough winter coat shed out to a satin-smooth finish. His dapples were less pronounced this year, and his general silver-gray color had lightened considerably. He covered the rough land as though mounted on soft but powerful springs. His unflagging stride swept the miles behind him.

One warm day, he sensed that he was almost home. He could

smell it in the breeze. He came upon the last mark of civilization, a low ranchhouse nestling in a grove of willow trees at the end of a long valley. Cloud could see no humans about but he swerved west, then turned north again, in order to avoid the chance of meeting any.

By now, the snowline had climbed up into the thick timber, then on above the timberline, leaving in its wake grass that was thick and green in the spring sunshine.

Looking upward from the valley, Cloud could see a band of mares and foals feeding on the velvety mountainside. He recognized this as the area where he had lived, and the air was laden with the familiar scents of horses he had known. Their number had diminished considerably since he had left them, three years ago. During that time, they had been relentlessly pursued, for the human horde was seemingly bent on their annihilation. Many mustangs had been captured and a number of them had been shot.

The gray sire who had led and protected Cloud was nowhere to be seen. But high on a rocky ledge, to the right of the grazing horses, boldly etched against the sky, stood a magnificent sorrel stallion.

Cloud was urged on by the scent of the mares. He hardly glanced at the red horse, but the instant the sorrel caught sight of the gray, he came sliding down the steep slope to meet the intruder. His tail and head were up, his nostrils quivered with rage as he challenged the gray stallion with a shrill, piercing whistle that lifted the mares' heads and caused the foals to stop their frolicking to see what this was all about. Cloud too had witnessed stallions fighting, when he was a baby at his mother's side. Now his life had come full circle, for he was back in home territory once more, advancing toward his own encounter.

Head low, he went charging upgrade in long jumps to face the red challenger. The two stallions came together fifty yards below the crest of the steep bluff. The collision of their meeting sent both horses down the incline, rolling over and over in the boiling dust.

As Cloud twisted convulsively to regain his feet, one sharp hoof of his opponent opened a wide gash along his shoulder. Locked together like wrestlers, the two lurched to their hind legs, searching for an opening, with mouths open and teeth bared. A pair of rabbits scurried from underfoot and went bounding away to escape the raging battle. The stallions had become like two dragons in combat, striking, slashing, squealing with fury.

Cloud carried the attack. All the pain and frustrations of his past rodeo career stormed unmercifully against his opponent. At last there was something of flesh and blood at which he could strike. This was not a rope or a saddle or a man too smart to get within reach. Here was a creature he could understand and cope with.

The fighting horses were evenly matched. What Cloud lacked in weight, he made up for in agility. His months in rodeo had taught him how to buck and twist and swap ends with an alacrity that had left many a rider sitting up there in the sky. Now the gray was using all his past experiences with vehemence.

The sorrel finally fell back before this onslaught. He was a veteran of many a duel, but never before had he faced anything like this. He was unable to set himself in a position to counterattack. Now he was continuously on the defensive and a battle could not be won that way. His neck and shoulders were crisscrossed by the wounds Cloud was inflicting on him. He was beginning to stagger. Once, he went down to his knees but, somehow, managed to recover. As the combat ripped its way down into the valley, huge flocks of butterflies rose before it, soaring above the clouds of dust that enveloped this struggle for supremacy.

Suddenly, the sorrel decided that he had had enough. He left the scene of battle, with Cloud in close pursuit, nipping his hindquarters at every stride.

In a little while, Cloud came trotting back to the mares and foals, who had resumed feeding. He walked confidently among the animals, to let them see who their chief was now.

He was tired. The blood on his wounds had coagulated and the sweat was matting on both sides of his arched neck. He found a sandy pit and rolled, then sprang to his feet and shook himself vigorously.

The gray stallion took up his lookout station where the sorrel had stood only an hour before. He raised his muzzle and neighed shrilly again and again.

Part Two

10

THE blue Volkswagen bus was traveling painfully north. Six days ago, it had left New York State and today it was being buffeted broadside by a powerful, hot west wind in Wyoming. In the driver's seat, Jane Whiteside gripped the wheel tightly, trying to keep the car on course. Beside her sat her son, Lon, with one hand braced on the dashboard and the other clutching the saftey belt that cut across his middle.

"Hang in there, Mom!" He smiled over at his mother, "Only four hundred miles more to go."

The bus was heavily loaded, which helped keep it on the road. All their belongings were stacked behind them or tied down to the roof. They traveled slowly. Fifteen-year-old Lon had never seen so many back ends of passing automobiles while motoring. Wyoming appeared bare and stark compared to the green woodland and countryside of New York State. Millbrook, located in the beautiful Harlem Valley, where they had lived, seemed a million miles away, and the six days since they had left more like six months.

When his mother sold the boarding stable, which she and his father had operated since Lon could remember, the boy had felt as if the end of the world had come. He loved the life he had lived—the horse shows, the fox hunting, the trail riding. He didn't own a horse of his own but he had worked and schooled the boarders under his father's supervision.

"Now there was a horseman!" The dull ache in Lon's throat grew more painful, as he relived those awful moments when the news came of the horse van crash and his father's death. On that very same day, his mother received word that her father had been hospitalized in Montana with pneumonia. She went out to stay with him until he was well enough to get back to his ranch.

After she returned, three weeks later, she tried to keep things going at the stable for almost a year, but it became too much. Lon was in school a large part of the time, and good help was difficult to find. When Tom Richardson finally persuaded his daughter to sell the place and come live with him on his Montana cattle ranch, Lon was dismayed. Most people are reluctant to part with the things with which they are familiar—especially if they love them devotedly—to take up a new life about which they know nothing. It is never easy to start making close friends all over again. But it certainly was a challenge, his mother had pointed out to him.

Since his father's death, Lon had changed considerably from the happy, outgoing boy he had been. Now he did his school work and rode the horses faithfully but automatically. A deep depression had invaded his spirit and robbed him of his natural enthusiasm. This provided a strong added incentive for his mother to sell out and go West. Perhaps the big sky country would pull Lon out of his sorrow and sharpen his zest for living again. At least she hoped so.

That evening, the Whitesides stopped for the night at a small motel in Casper, Wyoming. From the window of his room, Lon could see the Big Horn Mountains, rising above the mesa. The sun had already gone down and the entire landscape was immersed in a pink afterglow. How solemn it all seemed!

"Great, isn't it?" his mother said softly, over his shoulder. "This is the country I grew up in. I remember once, when I was a little girl, I came down here with my mother and father in our old station wagon. It was my twelfth birthday. We had dinner in the Longhorn Restaurant, over there across the road. Later, we went to a movie, then sat in the car and ate the birthday cake my mother had baked at home."

She told Lon much more about growing up in this big country. So many happenings—joyful and sad. She was Janey Richardson, then. "Big Tom's girl," the neighbors called her. And she was daddy's girl until she fell in love with happy-go-lucky Dave Whiteside, foreman of the nearby Lazy H. When she was still in high school, they planned to marry and build a ranch of their own, but the war came and Dave joined the Marines.

She recalled the endless war years—the terrible battles in the Pacific, the anxiety, the letters of hope, the longing and waiting. At last Dave came home and they were married.

Memories came flooding back—spreading over the past. Those were difficult times, trying to keep the ranch going, with cattle prices going down—down.

Dave had become restless and discontented.

"Let's sell out and go East!" he exclaimed one evening after dinner. "I think I've got a buyer for the place—a fellow from Wisconsin who likes cows—and you know, Jane, it has always been horses with me."

His voice rose with enthusiasm. "I've been reading about New York State, Pennsylvania, and Connecticut—that area is loaded with horse shows and fox hunting and wealthy people who pay high prices for good horses. I know we can do all right there. What do you say?"

She wanted Dave to be happy, but her father was completely against the whole idea. "This is the country and the way of life you know!" he pleaded with his son-in-law. "Stay here and come in with me. We'll do all right!"

But Dave Whiteside would not listen. He was headstrong and resented his father-inlaw's interference. There were rising tempers and irretrievable hot words flung out in the heat of anger.

When the young couple left for the East, only Jane's mother went to the railway station to see them off.

"Dad will get over it," she comforted her daughter. But it was quite awhile before he did.

The boy and his mother stood there quietly in the twilight. Finally, she broke the silence. "We'll get there tomorrow. Your dad and I returned here only once, when my mother died. That was before you were born." A frown flitted across her brow, then a small smile touched her lips. "You know, Lon, your grandfather has never seen you."

Lon wondered what his grandfather would look like. He had pictures of him when he was young, a tall, lanky fellow, with flashing dark eyes. In the early days, he had been a mustanger, hunting wild horses for a living. But something had occurred that made him give it up. Lon's mother said he never talked about it and she had not been able to find out what it was from anyone. The family had been living in a tiny house on the outskirts of Warren, Montana, then. But after that, he took out a bank loan and bought a small cattle ranch at the foot of the Pryor Mountains, between the Yellowstone and Bighorn Rivers, in southern Montana. He settled down there with his wife and child. She had been just a little girl then. And Tom Richardson never ran mustangs again.

Shortly after dawn the next day, Lon and his mother were on the road again. They still had almost three hundred miles to go. They ate their breakfast en route—an orange, cold ham on white bread, and coffee.

After they crossed the Powder River, going west, they swung toward the north at Shoshoni. In Cheyenne, the country had been pretty flat, but here there were high green mesas and mountains everywhere. The weather had cooled considerably, too.

They drove through Kirby, Winchester, Worland, and Graybull. This had been the land of the Sioux and Sitting Bull, the Crow, the Cheyenne. Historic people, places, and events came swarming in on Lon, breaking through his wall of sorrow. Off to his right flowed the Big Horn River and beyond that the Big Horn Mountains. He began to sit up and take notice of things and ask questions about the land they were going through. He saw small groups of white-faced cattle, and cowboys on tough little horses hazing them along. Shortly after they crossed the border into Montana his mother stopped the car and waved an arm toward a range of hills that paralleled the road to the east. "Look there," she cried, "mustangs. Wild horses!"

Lon would never forget the sight of those running mustangs.

He had grown up with horses—hunters, jumpers, Thoroughbred types. But he had never seen anything like this. These horses were wild and untamed, had never known bits in their mouths or saddles on their backs. They were free as the wind—untouched by man. Their manes and tails fluttered like banners as they galloped along the crest of the hill.

Lon's heart skipped a beat as the band crossed the ridge. For an instant, their stallion leader stopped there to make sure all was well. His chestnut coat seemed on fire in the afternoon sunshine before he plunged out of sight after his departing herd.

A long, whistling breath escaped the boy's lips. "Wow!" was all he could manage to say.

The two weary travelers reached the ranch after dark. Lon had drifted off to sleep, waking only periodically after a bump or a sudden turn in the road.

His mother's hand on his shoulder woke him. "We're here, Son. Wake up!"

He opened his eyes to a rustic ranchhouse, low and rambling. In the glare of their car's headlights, it appeared to be pale brown in color against the black night. The door opened and the figure of a man appeared in the doorway, silhouetted against the soft glow behind him.

"Jane, is that you?" he called out.

"Yes, Dad," Lon's mother answered cheerfully. "We made it!" She and her father embraced for a long moment on the dirt walk in front of the porch steps. . . . When she finally turned to her son, her eyes were shining with tears.

"Dad," she said in a low voice. Her throat was tight and the words came through with difficulty. "This is Lon."

The boy and his grandfather solemnly shook hands. The latter's back was to the light, so Lon could not see his face, but the grandfather had a chance to study the boy's pale, drawn features and dark, haunted eyes.

"Let's get inside," he suggested briskly. "You fellows must be starved."

The three entered a large, low-ceilinged room. Stained flowered curtains, which Jane remembered her mother had made, framed four long windows. They had probably not been laundered since her death, she thought. An electric stove and oven combination and a stainless steel sink occupied one side of the room and a magnificent fieldstone fireplace was built against the opposite wall. In between were a scattering of rugs, a long oak table and half dozen wooden, straight-backed chairs. On the wall was an assortment of framed photographs—Jane growing up, her first pony. Her high-school graduation picture hung next to one of her parents with Jane in the middle, all smiling broadly at the camera. Below the rifle rack, which cradled a Winchester 44 and a 12 gauge shotgun, were more pictures of horses and cowboys yellowed with age. Above the fireplace was a set of moose antlers which dominated the entire room.

Here, Lon and his mother met Ralph Ramstadt, who helped run the ranch. He was tall, with thin blond hair and a pleasant, crooked smile. He and Tom Richardson looked enough alike to be father and son. The older man's face was more deeply lined and his hair was white, but both were lean and tall and hard. The color of their skins and the squint of their dark eyes had been indelibly stamped on their features by the sun and the wind of this big country. But their years in the saddle had given them straight backs and bowed legs that were much more at home on a horse than on the ground.

A black and white Alaskan Malamute was standing alertly in the middle of the big room. His brown eyes kept shifting appraisingly from Lon to his mother. His tail began to wag slowly when Tom Richardson proudly introduced him.

"Meet Bridger, the best darn dog I ever had."

Lon held out the back of his hand and Bridger stepped forward to sniff it. Evidently, it told him what he wished to know, for he moved in nearer and sat down beside the boy. He closed his eyes happily when Lon began scratching between his ears.

"I guess you're OK with him." Lon's grandfather nodded approvingly.

During the supper of grilled steak, fried potatoes, and hot mince pie, Lon quietly listened to the others while he stroked the top of Bridger's head. Mrs. Whiteside complimented the cooking, adding that the two men should eat more green vegetables. Ralph agreed but replied that cooking was simpler this way, especially when they did it themselves. Once a week, a cleaning woman came in to tidy up the place but, for the most part, they "batched it" alone. During the spring and fall roundup, Tom Richardson put on extra hands, but this was June and, except for riding fence, there was little to do. Lon's apathy was broken when the table talk turned to cattle and horses. His mother mentioned the wild mustangs they had seen near the Montana border.

"We have a band running near her," Ralph told her. "Only last week they were down this way, but most of the time they range through the Pryor Mountains, to the north."

"Are they really wild?" Lon asked.

Ralph leaned back in his chair and lit his pipe. "They are as wild and as untamed as wolves. The band I'm referring to is led by one terrific gray stallion. We call him Cloud and, believe me, he's just about as hard to catch as one."

He grinned over at his employer. "What do you think, Tom? Isn't he as beautiful a hunk of horse as you ever did see?"

Lon's grandfather nodded in agreement. "He sure is, but, a long time ago, I knew one other horse who was just as great looking. That horse was—" He cut short what he was about to say and rose to his feet abruptly. "Well, guess it's time to hit the hay," he suggested. "You two must be tired and we have a busy day ahead tomorrow." He laid a gentle hand on his grandson's shoulder. "See you in the morning, Lon. We must get you outfitted, and Ralph will show you the ropes around here."

Later, lying in bed, Lon could see the moon through the branches of the willow trees that surrounded the house. He was tired, but his blood was too stirred up for him to sleep. He kept thinking about the mustangs running wild and untamed, but most of all, it was their leader, Cloud, the gray stallion, that fired his imagination.

11

LON was up at dawn, eager to explore his new surroundings. There was a cluster of corrals to the rear of the house. Back home in Millbrook, they were called paddocks. Beyond the corrals was a barn, and Lon headed in that direction, knowing this was where he would find horses. Bridger trotted up ahead, glancing back to make sure the boy was following. As Lon turned into the doorway, he came face to face with Ralph, who was on his way out, carrying a bucket of milk. Two cats trailed along behind him.

"Hi, Lon!" he greeted the boy. "If you wait until I take this up to the house, I'll show you around."

"I'll carry it," Lon offered quickly, glad to be of some use.

Ralph handed over the milk pail with an approving smile. The cats followed all the way and scooted in behind the boy as the screen door shut. He placed the milk on the counter beside the kitchen sink. His mother was frying bacon.

"Don't go far," she called after her son as he left the room to rejoin Ralph. "Breakfast will be on in ten minutes."

Ralph was waiting outside and, together, the man and the boy strolled down to one of the corrals. A buckskin horse was standing in one corner, munching at a pile of hay.

"He's going to be yours," Ralph announced. "You'll like him. He can go all day and after supper."

Lon slid in between the rails and approached the buckskin. He was a far cry from the Thoroughbred types with which the boy had grown up. Lon judged he was maybe fifteen hands, and compact. He had good hindquarters and a short back, with a fine neck and head that indicated good breeding.

"He's a quarter horse," volunteered Ralph, as if reading Lon's thoughts. "Your grandfather bought him especially for you when he learned you were coming out here." He laid a hand on the horse's shoulder. "We call him Bucky. He's five years old—got a lot of cow sense, too, and as honest a roping horse as I ever did see."

"Gosh, he looks great!" exclaimed Lon. But he really didn't mean it. His eyes had been trained on the run-and-jump kind of horse, and Bucky was obviously no jumper.

After a leisurely breakfast of bacon and eggs, Lon's mother packed meat sandwiches for Ralph and her son and watched them ride out the drive together. Ralph was on a neat, compact bay horse and the boy was astride Bucky. The little horse pranced as they went through the gate. They checked fence line all morning and at noon, they ate their lunch in the shade of a clump of willows. Their horses grazed close by. Ralph pointed out the Pryor Mountains to the north.

"That's where the wild ones run. That mountain country is pretty rough and dry, covered with sage, but the land eases into red hills and then becomes a plain where we run most of our cattle."

Lon soon learned that Ralph possessed a tremendous knowledge of the history of this country, and, as they sat there watching the shadows lengthen in the afternoon, he painted for Lon a mural of the past the boy would never forget.

He told of the thousands of buffalo which had roamed here and the advent of the buffalo hunters, professional killers, who slaughtered the herds from a distance with .50 caliber rifles, solely for their skins. The wholesale, wildly wasteful destruction of the animals shocked and angered the Indians.

They fought and soon learned the kind of enemy they confronted, armed with powerful weapons, great in numbers, cold-blooded in killing. There was General Custer, who led his troops into Sitting Bull's camp at the Little Big Horn and got them massacred to the last man.

"That happened just north of the Pryor Mountains, not too far from where we are sitting right now," Ralph continued.

"Let's see, it was June 25, 1876, and this is 1968, which makes it almost one hundred years ago."

Ralph rose to his feet and hitched up his belt, "Funny thing, Lon." He spoke through clenched teeth. "it is typical of the thinking of most white men of the time that, when General Custer and his cavalry were wiped out because they attacked superior numbers, it was called 'The Custer Massacre.' But when these Sioux with their women and children were murdered in their tents, it was called 'The Battle of Wounded Knee.' "

On the way back to the ranch house, Ralph told Lon about a recent development that was alarming his grandfather and most of the other ranch people in the area. He said that, back in 1954, the Montana Bureau of Land Management had announced that the two hundred wild horses they calculated were living in the Pryor Mountains had been marked for roundup and auction. Ralph and Tom Richardson and many ranchers around Laurel and Billings, Montana, did not take this decision lying down, for they long had regarded the wild herd as a symbol of the "Old West." By strongly protesting the action at a series of public hearings, they were able to block the plan temporarily.

"But last month," continued Ralph, "the Bureau of Land Management announced that it was going ahead with its plan. Two weeks ago, we organized the Pryor Mountain Wild Horse Association and elected your grandfather its president. Now we are working like all get out to see what we can do to stop the extermination of these mustangs . . . but it looks pretty hopeless."

"But why?" asked Lon. "Why does the government want to do this? It sounds awful to me."

" It *is* awful. They insist that the horses have overgrazed their habitat and would face starvation if they are not removed," Ralph answered. "But that's a lot of hogwash. Wait till you have a good look at them. Sure they're small but they're in great shape. You'll get a chance to see for yourself."

Lon did get a chance to see for himself one morning almost a week later. By this time, he was accustomed to riding a stock saddle. It was quite different in shape and much heavier in weight than his Pariani jumping saddle, but it was extremely comfortable for riding long distances. And, as Ralph explained, "This saddle is built for ranch work. Dally a rope around that saddle horn and you can hold a 1,500-pound steer with no trouble."

Lon had been riding for an hour when he climbed the last fifty yards of a long slope. Then he saw them—mustangs, grazing a mile away on a dusty hillside, with nothing breaking the stillness but the chattering crickets and scurrying sage hens. The horses were all the colors of the West—dun, sorrel red, black, mouse gray, dappled, chestnut brown, creamy palomino. Something—maybe his scent, perhaps a sound—lifted their attention from the stunted grass they were grazing and they froze for a long minute, alert, sniffing, all their heads turned at the same angle.

The gray stallion in charge took a few tentative steps, snorted a warning, and pranced nervously around his band. The mares and foals began to stir. The hillside came slowly to life with a soft, rustling sound, as hoofs brushed the sage. The gray stallion whinnied a command and took a few quick nips at the mares' flanks. The foals moved to their mothers' sides. In another five seconds, the hillside erupted in dust. The band was

on the move at top speed. Wild-eyed and snorting, they trampled the foliage in their path, bound together by fear and the instinct for flight. The dust, rolling thickly up from the ground, covered their retreat. The stallion, guarding the rear, turned from time to time to watch for pursuit.

Lon sat frozen on his horse, not daring to move a muscle. The wild band reached the ridgeline and disappeared over the other side. The sound of the hoofbeats faded away.

For a moment, it was absolutely still. Then the crickets resumed their chorus, and, to Lon, it was almost as if he had dreamed what he had just seen. Mustangs! The word itself had a fine, hard western edge to it, half romance and half rawhide, thoroughly American. It was marvelous to feel that mustangs still roamed here, under an endless sky, living from year to year on what they could tear from the earth.

During the weeks that followed, his grandfather told Lon much about the mustangs. Once their ancestors had freckled the prairie for a thousand miles and more. Now they lived in the isolated wastelands that defeat most other animals. Once they could be counted in the millions. Now there were perhaps only ten thousand, warily loping over the ridges, away from the closing tide of civilization.

One evening, while sitting on the porch steps, Tom Richardson had told Lon about the wild horses that had filled the western horizon in the nineteenth century. They were descended from the animals brought to America by the colonists and the Spanish conquistadors. Originally, they were small, short-backed and sturdy. Nearly all of the present-day wild horses had no distinguishing physical features, other than the battered scruffiness resulting from an always chancy struggle

on the move at top speed. Wild-eyed and snorting, they trampled the foliage in their path, bound together by fear and the instinct for flight. The dust, rolling thickly up from the ground, covered their retreat. The stallion, guarding the rear, turned from time to time to watch for pursuit.

Lon sat frozen on his horse, not daring to move a muscle. The wild band reached the ridgeline and disappeared over the other side. The sound of the hoofbeats faded away.

For a moment, it was absolutely still. Then the crickets resumed their chorus, and, to Lon, it was almost as if he had dreamed what he had just seen. Mustangs! The word itself had a fine, hard western edge to it, half romance and half rawhide, thoroughly American. It was marvelous to feel that mustangs still roamed here, under an endless sky, living from year to year on what they could tear from the earth.

During the weeks that followed, his grandfather told Lon much about the mustangs. Once their ancestors had freckled the prairie for a thousand miles and more. Now they lived in the isolated wastelands that defeat most other animals. Once they could be counted in the millions. Now there were perhaps only ten thousand, warily loping over the ridges, away from the closing tide of civilization.

One evening, while sitting on the porch steps, Tom Richardson had told Lon about the wild horses that had filled the western horizon in the nineteenth century. They were descended from the animals brought to America by the colonists and the Spanish conquistadors. Originally, they were small, short-backed and sturdy. Nearly all of the present-day wild horses had no distinguishing physical features, other than the battered scruffiness resulting from an always chancy struggle for food and water. But every once in awhile, there was a throwback, such as Cloud, who possessed all the breedy qualities of his Arabian ancestors.

The mustangs flourished or declined as men had reason to use or ignore them. In the beginning, they were captured to make riding mounts, or rodeo broncs, or perhaps to be crossbred to produce draft animals. But the biggest demand came from the pet food industry, which had reduced their number from 150,000 to 25,000 in the 1930's.

"For sport, profit, or both," his grandfather had continued, "men have always chased them. I was one of them myself—a mustanger. When I would see a particular wild horse I liked, I would go through hell and high water to catch him. There's a saying in the West that there is nothing so good for the inside of a man as the outside of a horse. I guess it's bred right into him."

Some nights, by the fireside, Tom Richardson related the legends that had gathered around the mustangs, such as the one about the great white stallion that could pace faster than any other horse could gallop.

Then there were the tales about the defiant stallions that had leaped off cliffs rather than be taken; the ex-slave who had "turned mustang" and run with the horses, racing across the prairie with them and sleeping fitfully with them at night. Such legends, like the horses, were vanishing.

Lon loved his grandfather's story of how once, during his mustanging days, back around 1925, he had watched a black stallion tentatively test the ground around a water-hole corral for several days, and then, in a frenzy for water, impulsive rush into the trap set there. No sooner had he begun to drink than he heard the corral gate drop with a thud. He knew without a backward glance what had happened, but he finished quenching his thirst. After that, with one incredible leap, he had cleared the nine-foot corral wall and was gone!

"Now the only regrets I have," the old horseman confessed one night, "are for the ones that didn't get away. The satisfaction that I'd feel at catching some wise bunch didn't last long when I remembered that they'd be shipped, put to work, and starved into being good by some hombre who was afraid of them and didn't savvy them at all. More and more, I realized that they really belonged, not to man, but to the country of junipers and sages, of deep arroyos and freedom."

Lon and his mother knew that it was more than this general feeling which had made Tom Richardson give up mustanging. Something definite and devastating must have happened that he did not wish to talk about. Evidently, a nagging pain still lingered in his heart, for, every once in a while, when he recounted his adventures with the wild horses, it showed in his eyes. Perhaps some day, Lon hoped, he would find out what it was.

12

THE summer rolled by swiftly. Lon was steadily becoming himself again. As he absorbed more and more of this shining land, his natural spirit and exuberance returned. He found he loved everything about this new environment—the smell of the sage, the summer storms and the velvet hills, the sunsets and sunrises. He liked the morning best and always looked forward to the tantalizing aroma of cooking bacon when he came up to the house with Ralph after the barn chores were finished. The two had become great friends. The older man promptly took Lon under his wing. He taught him how to rope and ride western, which the boy learned very quickly. His background of jumping horses made the switch easy.

Bucky was no jumper but he safely carried Lon down perilous slopes, sliding on his hindquarters. The pair climbed mountains together and once they swam across the Big Horn River. At first, Lon was reluctant to admit that Bucky was quite a horse but, after a while, he was the first to crow about the buckskin's achievements. Lon had adapted to this new way of life with no reservations.

His mother too, adjusted readily to the routines on her father's cattle ranch. To see her son so contented gave her an ease and fullness of heart she had not felt in many months. It was wonderful to be home again, in the land of her birth. Of course, many modern innovations had been introduced, but the spirit was relatively unchanged since she was a little girl, and now she was beginning to observe the countryside all over again through the eyes of her son, and she was at peace with the world.

Mrs. Whiteside still had friends in southern Montana. Now old relationships were quickly picked up again. Among other things, she joined the Pryor Mountain Wild Horse Association.

In September, the cattle roundup began. Two extra hands were hired to help gather together the herd, which was spread out through the numerous valleys that swung northward.

One afternoon, Lon was riding slowly through the Pryor Mountains, on the lookout for strays. Ralph believed a couple of cows had drifted up that way and had the boy sent out to find them. Bridger loped on ahead for, besides being a good companion, he was an excellent cow dog. Tom Richardson always said, "If there's a cow within five miles, Bridger will find her."

The explosive roar of its engine sounded one split second after the low-flying aircraft came into view. The buckskin pony squatted, then scooted ahead so fast it seemed as though his hind legs would overrun the front ones. Lon desperately clutched the saddlehorn, as horse and rider plunged down the mountainside. Behind him came a band of mustangs, like an avalanche. They had appeared as suddenly as the airplane. The boy let out a long "HO-O-O!" when they swept past him, but it was drowned out by the pounding hoofs and choking dust and the ear-splitting sound of the motor as the aircraft banked to the left and came around for another pass at the panic-stricken horses. Lon was braced against the cantle of the saddle. His right arm was up to shield his face from the flying bits of stone. His left hand held the reins, trying to steady his pony. It was impossible to stop. Their momentum and the loose shale underfoot carried the pair helplessly downward behind the fleeing mustangs.

The heavens vibrated as the plane came over again, lower this time. Lon could hear the wind whistling through the wing struts. He did not dare look up, for he had all he could do to watch out below.

Ride it out, he told himself. Be still. Don't panic. Don't rock the boat. One misstep can mean a broken neck.

The little buckskin was barreling along over a maze of rocks and boulders as if he were a mountain goat. There was no room for mistakes and Bucky made none. At last, the land emerged into the open. Up ahead, the mustangs were fanning out and slowing down. But the airplane relentlessly zoomed in once more. A screaming siren was swinging from the end of a long line attached below the landing gear, driving on the already exhausted horses.

Lon was finally able to pull up his blowing pony and turn away from the tragedy unfolding below. He knew what was about to happen. Ralph had told him about this cruel performance that had been going on for the past couple of years. The whole operation sickened and disgusted the boy. As soon as the fleeing wild mustangs reached the level going of the flats, a truck would take off after them. Men standing on the truck

bed would rope them, one by one. The trailing end of each lasso was tied to a hundred-pound tire, and the poor captive creature would run, dragging the tire behind him, until his legs or his heart gave out.

When the mustangers drove up to load their victims, those animals still able to stand would be swaying helplessly with the effort of their labored breathing. They were jammed roughly into trucks and driven off—to be slaughtered for dog and cat meat. In all his years of living with and learning about horses, Lon had never witnessed anything as cruel as this.

Ralph had described other forms of cruelty the mustangers used. In the Wyoming Red Desert, near Rock Springs, mares captured by mustangers were gentled and then released to run again with the wild herds, but not until their nostrils had been sewed almost completely shut with rawhide rope or pinched together with barbed wire.

In this pitiful condition, a mare would live all year on the hot desert with her nostril flare so restricted that she was unable to draw a full breath of air. Thus handicapped, she would act as a brake on the band, slowing the pace of the entire herd and making them an easy prey for the men who hunted them the following spring.

Another method employed by horse runners in that region to slow down the fleet-footed mustangs was to bend a horseshoe around the ankle of a mare and release her with the wild band. The bent horseshoe would not hurt her when she walked, but it would strike and bruise her legs whenever she began to run.

"A lot of wild horses," said Ralph, "take getaway trails that no man could ride and there is no way riders can turn a bunch unless they do something like this to handicap the mustangs' efforts to escape."

As it is a Federal offense to run wild unbranded horses with aircraft on public lands, Ralph had asked one mustanger why he continued to do it. "Well," replied the man, "how else am I going to catch the horses? They now live in such remote places that you would never get what's still out there on horseback."

"If they now live in such remote places," Ralph had continued to question the mustanger, "why not just leave them there?"

The blunt reply was, "Why leave them there? What good are they?"

Lon was thinking about these things while he and his pony were gradually working their way back up the mountainside down which they had just come in such haste. Bridger rejoined them. When the fireworks had begun, the dog had sought refuge on the top of a boulder and stayed there until the air cleared. The dust was beginning to settle now and, again, the strong minty odor of sage permeated the wind. Lon breathed deeply of the cool breeze blowing down from the Pryors. He looked appreciatively at the craggy slopes—golden ochre in the afternoon sunshine.

Suddenly, Bridger stopped in his tracks. His head had come up and a deep growl rumbled in his chest. Then he barked sharply and glanced back over his shoulder.

"What is it, boy?" Lon asked.

The Malamute advanced with his head lowered. Lon legged his horse forward. Bridger was all caution now—on his toes. Bucky checked to a halt, tossed his head nervously, and snorted.

There was something out of the ordinary up there, Lon felt sure. He slipped from the saddle, dropped the reins over his pony's head, and made his way upward on foot. He rounded a jutting shelf of rock with his hand on Bridger's collar and there, just ahead and to the right of him, wedged tightly up against a boulder, lay a horse. The animal raised his head and, for one unforgettable moment, the boy's gaze was held by the liquid brown eyes of the gray mustang.

Lon recognized the stallion instantly. He could not believe his good fortune! Here he was, face to face with a horse he had admired and coveted ever since he had arrived at his grandfather's ranch. How often, stretched out flat on his stomach, he had studied through his field glasses every line and contour of this superb animal.

Even lying there, his body crusted with sweat and dust, the horse was beautiful. Lon realized instantly what must have happened. The gray stallion, bringing up the rear of the running mares and unable to see the ground they were speeding over because of the dust, evidently had stepped in a hole and gone down. He had probably slammed up against the big boulder and knocked himself cold. He was just coming to when Lon spotted him. As soon as he found he was wedged tightly between the big rock and the slope, he would start thrashing about to free himself. Lon did not know how badly the mustang was hurt, but he did know that, if he didn't get him out in a hurry, the stallion would struggle to escape until he was dead. Horses will do this. His grandfather had told him that, only the summer before, his favorite cow pony had killed himself trying to get out of a watering trough into which he had accidently fallen.

There was not a moment to lose. Lon rushed back to his pony and vaulted into the saddle, uncoiling his lariat even as they lunged up to where the stallion lay. He swung down to the ground and quickly fashioned a halter around the dazed stallion's head. Back in the saddle, he dallied the rope to the saddlehorn.

"Let's go, Bucky," he said softly.

The rope tightened and vibrated as the pony drove his weight against it. The gray stallion slid slowly forward. He was in the clear now but made no attempt to get up.

Dismounting, Lon left Bucky where he was and returned to the mustang. He hunched down beside him. Then, carefully placing one hand on the horse's shoulder, he coaxed, "Come on, my friend. You can make it now."

Cloud shuddered, as if ten thousand flies had suddenly descended upon him. His eyes went hollow like a cat's. His ears flattened. With a tremendous burst of energy, he lurched to his feet . . . staggered, but managed to remain upright, swaying.

Now Lon could see blood oozing from a deep gash just above the stallion's knee. He untied his kerchief and fashioned a pressure bandage around the wound.

There was no telling what the mustang would have done if he had been feeling himself, but, fortunately, he was still in shock. Lon tugged on the rope and the gray followed him. It surprised the boy that this wild horse led so easily. Of course, he had no way of knowing that Cloud was rope broke and reacted instinctively to the pull of the line.

Now, mounted on Bucky and leading the wounded horse slowly, Lon headed back to the ranch, Bridger trotting close by.

Sunset came, then night settled over the land. They stopped frequently to let the mustang rest. Lon changed the blood-soaked bandage twice, making good use of his shirttails. The stars came out as the four pushed on, with a cold north wind at their backs.

They were on a lonely dirt road when Lon noticed a pair of headlights coming toward him. Soon, a jeep pulled up, and Ralph and Mrs. Whiteside got out.

"Oh, Lon!" his mother's voice was shaking with anxiety,

"Where have you been? We were so worried!" She broke off when she spotted the gray mustang, standing in the gloom beyond the glare of the headlights.

Lon explained what had happened. It was finally agreed that the boy would continue leading the mustang in, while Ralph and his mother would hurry back to the ranch and telephone their veterinarian, Dr. Rosen, and get a place ready for the patient.

When Lon finally reached the ranch, about an hour later, he led Cloud into a corral, the one with the nine-foot sides and the shed in the corner. Dr. Rosen had arrived already, in his white truck, his hospital on wheels that contained everything—lab, refrigerator, and all sorts of instruments and tools and medications a veterinarian would possibly need for his wide variety of calls.

He skillfully stitched up the wound, then gave the horse a tetanus shot and a shot of antibiotics.

Dr. Rosen was a new vet in the area. He was a Cornell graduate who, all the neighboring ranchers agreed, "had a way with animals—especially sick ones. He treated all kinds of livestock, but horses were his particular love. He was a slim, dark-haired young man, with horn-rimmed glasses and a pleasant manner. He was not tall. Dr. Rosen liked to declare that this was the key to his success. "If I were a big guy," he would say with a laugh, "my patients would be suspicious, but because I'm not, they figure I'm harmless and trust me."

Of course, it was more than that. He was a warm-hearted, competent doctor, who loved his work and was completely fearless. This combination was hard to beat.

"Let him rest tonight," he told Lon. "Make sure he has plenty of hay and water. I'll look in on him tomorrow morning."

After he left, Lon stood outside the corral, watching his horse. Cloud ate a little and emptied his water bucket. Lon refilled it and placed it on the hook in the horses' shelter. Cloud swung his head around and laid back his ears when his captor came close, but the boy stood his ground for a minute or so . . . then he turned his back to the gray mustang and left him. He also checked Bucky, to make sure all was well with him, too, and rubbed down the little buckskin as he contentedly munched his hay.

After supper, Lon went back down to the corral to see how the gray stallion was doing. He found him resting in a bed of straw, like a big dog. The boy watched him for a long time until he heard his mother's voice behind him.

"It has been a tiring day," she reminded him quietly.

"It sure has," agreed Lon, "but what a great one!"

13

CLOUD ran a fever for five days. Dr. Rosen diagnosed his case as exhaustion and dehydration from being pursued constantly, with no time to drink. Horses can go for long periods without food but not without water. Besides his wound, he had a badly wrenched shoulder, a concussion and a cracked hoof.

The other wild horses in the Pryor Mountain Region were also having their troubles. The Montana Bureau of Land Management was erecting a huge trap around a main waterhole. It would be finished by the following summer, when the approximately two hundred wild horses running in the Region would be rounded up for auction.

Tom Richardson was up in arms about this. "Practically all those mustangs will go to the cannery," he declared indignantly. "What's more, that roundup will be a bloody massacre. You cannot run wild horses into the kind of corral the Bureau of Land Management men are making. You want one on the flat, where you can handle the horses. You don't want to build a trap they can commit suicide in. They will, you know. They'll just pile up in a corral on a steep hill like that. When a horse is panic stricken, he doesn't know what anything is. Those mustangs will jam around and break their legs and, by gosh, half of them will be killed before they can be separated for shipment and auction."

He and one other member of the Horse Protection Association went off, to confer with the Montana senators and congressmen in Washington and ask them to look into the inhumane matter and to intervene. They had little success, for the work steadily continued on the trap.

Cloud's wound healed satisfactorily and the soreness in his shoulder improved noticeably. The torn hoof would grow out in time.

Lon made no attempt to force his friendship with the stallion. His dad had once told him, "With a horse or any other animal, learn to wait patiently, and eventually he will come to you." Twice a day, the boy brought Cloud small portions of grain and dumped them on the ground beside the hay, but never once did he lay a hand on the mustang.

School began. Often, as the boy waited for the bus in the morning, he could see Cloud watching him between the bars of the corral. One afternoon, when he stepped off his bus, Cloud nickered a greeting. This marked the wild horse's first acknowledgment of his awareness of the boy.

That same evening, when Lon brought the usual portion of grain, he waited in the feeding corner of the corral for the horse to come and get it. The mustang approached the boy cautiously, then carefully reached his muzzle into the metal pan which Lon held with both hands.

The following morning, as Cloud munched his grain, Lon stroked his neck.

Later that week, Lon tried placing his hands on the mustang's back, then hanging his weight from them. At first, Cloud objected by sidling away but, within a few days, he learned to stand quietly.

One evening, Lon slid a saddle pad on the mustang and cinched it loosely into place. Cloud crow-hopped around the corral for almost three minutes, then stopped and swung his head around to sniff the object. His nose told him it was no bucking saddle and there was no flank strap behind it to annoy him. But he rolled in the dust on general principles—several times and shook himself like a dog when he got up.

Lon moved over to stand beside him, talking quietly.

"That wasn't so bad was it? Just takes a little getting used to, that's all."

He removed the pad, then reached up and scratched the horse between the ears. From his pocket, he brought out a handful of grain and fed it to the mustang.

"Pretty soon, I'll start getting you acquainted with a bit," the boy added.

The thought of one day riding Cloud filled Lon with a pleasure he could hardly describe. His mother and Ralph caught his enthusiasm. Only Tom Richardson hung back. He gave Lon no encouragement whatever. He was a man of great experience who had spent a good part of his life with wild horses; yet he never once offered Lon any advice.

As a matter of fact, he steered clear of any discussion concerning the gray mustang, and soon Lon also avoided any mention of the stallion in the presence of his grandfather.

In the meanwhile, there was a hopeful change coming to the status of the wild horses of the Pryor Mountain area. The Bureau of Land Management appointed a committee, composed

of eight authorities on wild game and the environment. Tom Richardson was one of these. It was announced that this committee would hold two meetings in the Pryor Mountain region, to view the horses and their habitat, one in the fall, and one in the early spring. No further action in capturing the mustangs would be taken until the Bureau received a full report from the authorities. Work on the trap was to stop. Tom Richardson went to Billings, Montana, for the first committee meeting. Among those in attendance were a number of members of the Rod and Gun Club, who vigorously protested leaving the horses in the Pryor Mountain area. "Our harvest of deer has fallen off!" they cried. "We want the horses out of there!"

But during this first meeting, an important fact came to light. A study regarding the decline in the deer population had not even been made in the Pryor Mountains. The count had been taken elsewhere in the state of Montana and was being used as misleading evidence that the wild horses were "over-competing" with the mule deer in the Pryor Mountain range. This fact absolved the horses from all responsibility for the decline. Even when the deer were later shown to be doing poorly in the Pryor Mountains, the situation, being general could hardly be blamed on the horses.

The Montana Bureau of Land Management also brought up the fact that the region was eroded and had deteriorated because of the mustangs. But one member of the committee, Dr. Wayne Cooper, an authority on range management, pointed out that the damage had been done fifty to one hundred years earlier and was the work of domestic sheep. The horses had not caused this condition, nor were they greatly aggravating it, except for the network of trails they had created in their long treks to water. If plastic tanks could be put into the region to catch rainwater, it would relieve the horses of the necessity of so much traveling in search of it. The trails, he felt, might even heal over.

The fall viewing was held in the middle of October. The mustangs appeared sleek and fat. The spring viewing would be the deciding factor.

That year, winter came blasting down with the worst snowstorms the natives could remember. For days at a time, the roads were impassable for the school buses or any other vehicles. Lon spent a good part of these days with the gray stallion. He introduced Cloud to grooming equipment, and the wild horse learned to stand as the boy curried his winter coat and brushed out his mane and tail. Lon even got to picking up the mustang's feet and rapping on them, in preparation for the day when he had the mustang shod.

"Wait until spring comes," he announced one night at the supper table. "I am going to ride that horse. I know he has been ridden before. There are white saddle marks on his whithers."

Ralph agreed. "But there is also a rubbed place on his flank where a bucking strap has been pulled tight," he added. "I'd venture to guess he has been a rodeo bronc at one time. Look how he accepts the rope and halter."

Lon glanced over at his grandfather, who had his eyes on his empty plate, the fingers of his right hand drumming softly on the table. "What do you think, Grandpa?" he asked. "Do you think Cloud was a rodeo bronc?"

Tom Richardson gazed over at his grandson, and, for a moment, it seemed as if he had something of importance to add to the discussion—but his answer to Lon's question was a noncommittal "Could be." There was a finality in his voice which plainly said, "Keep me out of it!"

I know he would like me to turn Cloud loose, Lon thought.

But why should I? I found him. I brought him home. I nursed him back to health. I love him. If I can get to ride him, maybe I could do some barrel racing. He's fast and quick turning. He might even make a show jumper or hunter.

These half-formed plans—and others—raced madly through Lon's mind. Besides, he rationalized, if I turn him loose, he is sure to be caught, sooner or later. Then he would only wind up in the cannery.

All winter long, while the friendship grew between Lon and the gray stallion, Tom Richardson made repeated trips to the state capital. And many a night, when Lon went to bed, he could see the light shining under his grandfather's bedroom door and knew he was in there, reading documents and writing numerous letters to politicians and conservationists everywhere, seeking help for the wild horses.

Lon came to admire his grandfather more and more for the man that he was and his wholehearted dedication to the cause of the mustangs.

Was that why the older man wanted Cloud to be free again? But were there also deeper reasons—too painful for him to talk about?

March finally came. As the snow melted, water ran in the gulleys once more, and the miracle of spring was on the land.

The committee met in Billings for the second time. When all arguments had been heard, the most impressive exhibit of all was photographic proof of the present conditions of the wild horses. At the fall viewing, the animals had looked to be in fine shape. Now, even in March, after an extra hard winter, although the mustangs looked thin from existing on scant feed, it was obvious to all on the committee that the Pryor Mountain herd was in no danger of starvation.

In June, the committee submitted its final report to Washington. The Department of the Interior adopted its unanimous recommendation that the Public Lands in the Pryor Mountains be retained for the use of wild horses above all purposes and be named the Pryor Mountain Wild Horse Refuge.

What a victory!

It was almost as if, in some way, Cloud had found out about these glad tidings. Or maybe it was the coming of spring again, with the sense of new life in the air—or perhaps it was because the gray horse was fully recovered from his injuries. Whatever the reason, of late the stallion spent most of his days in the north corner of his corral, gazing off at the distant hills. Occasionally, he would pace back and forth along the rails, stopping from time to time to rest his eyes longingly on the horizon.

One afternoon, sitting atop the corral fence, Lon watched the horse intently. His mind was troubled and torn with indecision. The establishment of the Pryor Mountain Wild Horse Refuge had not made things easier for him. Now he could no longer tell himself he was keeping the mustang for unselfish reasons—to save him from going to the cannery. Was he really depriving Cloud of his freedom? Besides, what is freedom, anyway? Lon asked himself the question. He thought he knew what it meant to humans, but what about the creatures of the wild? Most horses in the United States were not "creatures of the wild"—but did wild mustangs fit into the same category?

"He's getting more restless every day, isn't he?"

Lon turned and was surprised to see his grandfather standing there, also watching the gray horse.

The boy nodded and slid to the ground. His grandfather fell

in beside him as they walked back to the house. When they reached the front porch, Tom Richardson placed a restraining hand on Lon's shoulder.

"Come over here," he said softly. "There is something I want to talk to you about."

He motioned to the porch steps and they both sat down together. There was a long moment of awkward silence.

"This thing between you and the gray horse," his grandfather began. "I've kept pretty much out of it."

Lon stared straight ahead and made no comment.

"Well, I did keep out of it. I wanted no part of the whole thing." The older man hesitated, then went on with more determination. "But today as I watched you up there on the corral fence I had the feeling that I was somehow letting you down, that if there was something I could do to help I should do it, and not just sit back and let you fret all by yourself."

Lon sat up and faced his grandfather. He had been depressed all week. Seeing Cloud so agitated preyed on the boy's conscience because he felt completely responsible for the horse. Often he had considered asking his grandfather what he should do about the dilemma; yet at the same time he was half afraid of the answer he might get. But now his defenses were down and he waited with thumping heart for any help Tom Richardson might offer.

His grandfather cleared his throat. His voice became stronger as he began to speak once more.

"Lon, I'm going to tell you a story that I've never told to anybody. It has been with me for many years, but I'm going to tell it to you because it might help you understand why I feel the way I do about the mustangs. I know there are some who won't believe this story, but if you had ever chased wild horses

and seen what they will do to escape capture, you would be sure it happened.

"I was almost twenty-seven years old at the time. I had already bossed a herd of cattle, and had been mustanging for more than ten years. As you know, long ago, these wild horses were almost as numerous as the buffalo. Even when I was chasing them, you could count them by the hundreds. Sometimes, it would seem as if the whole side of a mountain was in motion, so covered was it with broomtails and so evenly were they moving.

"Of course, when I was mustanging, they were thinning in numbers, but they were getting so they wouldn't run at every small scare. They began to save their legs for a pinch. They got over running without reason and made sure a rider was really after them before they started. Then they would just move fast enough to keep at a safe distance.

"It was along the Medicine Bow River, in southern Wyoming, that I spotted a band of wild horses, led by a blood bay stallion with a jet black mane and tail. I tell you he was an eyeful, easily as beautiful as this Cloud horse. Well, I got six other mustangers to go with me to capture this band, all agreeing that I should have the bay stallion, if we ever got him within reach of a rope."

His grandfather paused for a moment. His eyes narrowed as his mind probed back to a time gone by. "In the beginning," he continued, "by using a good deal of patience and some running, we managed to work a gentle belled mare into the wild band. The stallion adopted her and the bell was a distinct help in dogging the herd at night.

"We followed the mustangs in a buckboard, drawn by a pair pair of tough ponies, which, with driver, were changed three times every twenty-four hours. The wild band kept on familiar prairie ground, circling Tecumseh Peak several times.

"Four days and nights, we kept so close behind them that they had little chance to eat, drink or rest. Abstinence perhaps helped them to endure. Water in quantities stiffens muscles and shortens wind. Finally, the mustangs were so nearly "walked down," we were able to move in and haze the wild bunch, together with some manageable horses, into a big cow pen.

"In the pen, the blood bay stallion showed up as beautiful, as well-proportioned, and as desirable as he had appeared racing away on the prairies. During the long chase, he had exercised much more than the other animals of his band, circling so often around them. Yet, standing there, gaunt and jaded, he still showed the fire of life. He was about four years old, an age at which any horse is comparatively green. I was sure he could have a great future with me.

"When roped, he struggled but did not fight. When mounted, he did not pitch, but I kept him in that pen for three days. On the fourth day, I decided to ride him out. I used a hackamore instead of a bridle. Tim Jacobs and George Peterson were on either side of me, to give me a hand in case I got into trouble. The bay went quietly enough. We headed for Jim Ned Creek, some distance off, for the crossing there was shallow, no more than eighteen inches deep. The reins of the hackamore were loose."

Tom Richardson's voice trembled as he relived his story. "When we hit the creek, the mustang thrust his muzzle into the water up to his eyes. Then, suddenly, he lay down, his muzzle still submerged.

"I quickly loosened his girth and tried to get him to his feet, but he would not move.

"'Tim! George! Help me!' I yelled. The three of us, struggling together in the water, could not get that horse's nostrils above the surface for air! I was on my knees, grappling with his head, but it was like an anchor that had jammed itself into the ocean floor. I punched him and screamed into his ear, but that horse would not submit, and he drowned himself right there."

His grandfather's voice broke. He stared down at his clenched fists, resting on his knees. When he looked at Lon again, he was composed, but his eyes were blurred with the dismal memory.

"Afterward, at night, I would dream I was in the water, wrestling with that mustang. I'd cry out in pain and frustration and I'd come awake with a start, the sweat pouring out of me. When I got to thinking on it, I began to realize what a precious thing freedom is. Students of horse behavior may give you a million reasons for what happened out there in Jim Ned Creek, but I know in my heart that taking that mustang's liberty from him also took his instinct for life."

Tom Richardson rose to his feet, walked away from the porch, and leaned against a willow tree. Lon followed and stood beside him. The man and the boy gazed at the distant hills with the red sun slipping down behind them and did not stir for a long time.

Finally, his grandfather took a deep breath and spoke to Lon. "After that, I vowed that I would never again, as long as I lived, deprive any living creature of his freedom."

Now Lon understood. All his questions had been answered at last—and all these answers had crystalized into what he must do.

14

LON woke just before dawn. He dressed quietly in the half light and, carrying his boots, walked softly through the house. He stopped in the kitchen and sliced off a hunk of bread, which he stuffed into his jacket pocket. Bridger sat in a corner, watching. "You stay," Lon whispered to the dog.

Outside, the cool dawn breeze rustled through the treetops. On the porch steps, the boy sat down to put on his boots. He zipped up his suede jacket as he strode swiftly toward the stable.

Bucky blinked when the lights came on. Lon saddled up. As he led the buckskin out, the eastern horizon was aglow with the coming sunrise.

Lon stopped at Cloud's corral and left the buckskin tied to a hitching post. The gray mustang was standing in the middle of the enclosure. His eyes were on Lon as the boy walked boldly up to him and slipped a rope halter over his ears. Tying the shank to a rail, Lon began grooming the mustang. He tried not to look at Cloud as he curried him vigorously. Brush next, then soft cloth, to bring out the silver highlights—even at this early hour.

When he finished, he led the stallion through the gate; then, still holding the lead rope, he mounted his pony and jogged down to the road, crossed over, and turned northwest, heading toward the Pryor Mountains.

This was Cloud's first time away since he had come to the ranch. He pranced as they moved along—tossing his head and snorting. The blood which had been dormant all winter began to surge through his veins with new promise.

The sun broke over the eastern horizon and the tops of the cliffs on Lon's left turned bright red-gold. The sunlight crept slowly down the rocky walls into the misty valley. It touched Lon's head, then warmed his body as it cut through the morning chill.

The trio traveled for two hours, heading northwest all the way. They passed through narrow ravines and over rocky outcrops—but continuously moved upgrade. They stopped once for all three to drink from a creek that gurgled noisily down a hillside, then continued on their way, advancing deeper and deeper into the Pryors. At noon, Lon munched his bread as he rode.

The day was clouding up. Long shadows lanced across the sweeping landscape, and, way off to the right, a rain cloud spread downward.

The gray stallion seemed fluorescent in the changing light. Just as a rainbow trout loses its brilliant color when taken out of the water, so Cloud had lost his sparkle in the past months. He had had wonderful care and the love of a boy, but the gray mustang was a creature of the wild, needing freedom as the trout needs the flowing water.

He seemed to grow larger and move more buoyantly. His eyes had a gleam that Lon had never seen in them before.

It was two o'clock in the afternoon when the three pulled up in the shadow of a giant bluff. Below them, the land reached out in all directions to a far-off line of purple hills.

Lon dropped his reins to the ground and dismounted. The sadness he had felt since hearing his grandfather's story was miraculously lifting from his spirit. He was sure of himself once more.

Cloud stood like a statue, his head pressed against the boy's chest. Lon took the gray muzzle between his hands and rested his cheek against the softly blowing nostrils.

"Good-by, my friend," he whispered. "God bless!" He reached up and pulled the halter off. Stepping back, he waved it gently at the gray mustang.

"Go on," he cried. "You're free—free!"

Cloud wheeled away and trotted off a few steps. He glanced back once, then rolled off into a smooth lope, down the hillside and across a shallow stream. The water sparkled like quicksilver as he splashed on through. On the far bank, he broke into a gallop, disappeared momentarily behind a rise of land, then emerged again, running faster, with his mane and tail streaming out behind him.

Lon stood beside his pony, watching until the gray mustang was lost in the distance. His heart was pounding as if he were out there with Cloud, running beside him. The wind was slapping against his eardrums, keeping time with the rhythmic beat of flying hoofs.

The boy turned away and swung up into the saddle. He gathered together the rope halter and shank and looped it over the horn, then legged Bucky back down the rocky trail.

The gray stallion loped out of an arroyo and pulled up on the edge of a wide, sweeping mesa. He had been running for more than an hour and was blowing hard. His long confinement had left him temporarily out of condition, but he was in good flesh and feeling great. Ahead, almost a mile away, he could see a band of mustangs grazing on a high rise of land.

Cloud's whinny echoed like the blast of a train whistle. The horses' heads came up as one—ears forward, pinpointing the direction from where it came. The gray stallion tossed his head. The wind lifted his mane and his tail arched upward as he galloped toward them.

ABOUT THE AUTHOR-ILLUSTRATOR

SAM SAVITT and horses have been inseparable practically all of his life. He has written numerous books about horses in all fields, from rodeo to the Maryland Hunt Cup Race. His illustrations have appeared in *Sports Illustrated, True, Boys' Life,* and other national magazines, as well as in over ninety books, several of which he wrote himself. His drawings and paintings of horses have been recognized as some of the finest in the United States.

Pennsylvania-born Sam Savitt and his wife now live on a small farm in North Salem, New York. His favorite pastime—when away from his drawing board—is riding and schooling horses.